DEATH BEGETS

PRAISE FOR MATHEW KAUFMAN

"*Death Begets* is a finely crafted and deeply unsettling collection of fictions in which we can hear the powerful, fearless voice of a writer who can create real characters, set in a world we can believe in. That the stories catch us in their grip is rooted in the emotion Mat lets his characters feel. He writes about the passions that inspire people and the fears that destroy them."

— CLIVE BARKER, AUTHOR OF IMAJICA, CABAL, THE
DAMNATION GAME, AND CREATOR OF HELLRAISER

"Kaufman's real life experiences infuse his work with unflinching power."

— MERCEDES M. YARDLEY, AUTHOR OF THE BRAM STOKER
AWARD-WINNING LITTLE DEAD RED

"The works of Mat Kaufman do not hit you in the face all at once, but rather tiptoe up your spine and burrow itself into your brain where it will eat at you, slowly, over time. There's nobody in the horror biz in his league, not even close. The dude scares me!"

— TIM CHIZMAR, AUTHOR OF SOUL TRAITOR, MODERN MADNESS

ALSO BY MATHEW KAUFMAN

DEATH BEGETS

MATHEW KAUFMAN

ISBN 978-1-7341311-0-9
ISBN: 1-7341311-0-1

For those who support me in all of my ventures. Russell, Vinny "Bunny", the Tylers, both tall and small, and Kady, the true source of hate! You guys are the best.

"I hate to advocate drugs, alcohol, violence, or insanity to anyone, but they've always worked for me."

-Hunter S. Thompson

LAUREL MOUNTAIN

"Welcome to Laurel Mountain Sanitarium, Mister...?" the man said, reaching out to shake his hand.

"Daggets. Frank Daggets," Frank said, accepting the hand. His arm quickly soaked with rain.

"I'm Frederick von Haussen, Superintendent of the facilities. Please, come inside. The rain can be most unpleasant," von Haussen replied.

Just then a flash of lightning shot across the storm-filled sky. It illuminated the tall stone building in a bluish white hue. The lightning flashed several more times. Thunder cracked through the air. It filled Frank's ears as he hunched at the sound and glanced up.

"Are you all right, Mr. Daggets? Surely you are not frightened of a bit of thunder. Laurel Mountain gets storms three- hundred plus days a year. Goodness. Let's get inside. "

Frank felt ridiculous after von Haussen caught his reaction to a bit of thunder. He tried his best to regain his composure. He climbed the thirteen stone steps that led to the large wooden doors of the entry way. Above the doors, carved in stone, read *"Laurel Mountain Sanitarium.* "The door was cracked; a guard watched the interaction and waited for von Haussen's return.

Once von Haussen reached the top step, the large wooden doors creaked open. Frank stepped inside, glad to be out of the downpour, but not glad to be inside this place. It was dark inside. Small yellow lights slightly illuminated the sanitarium walls. Frank looked at his new surroundings.

The welcome area was not much more than a red area rug bordered with gold embroidery. Large patches of fringe along the edge were missing. A small tube radio sat atop the table, an orange glow emitting from the dials. The opening of "The Lone Ranger" played quietly. Several well-worn wooden chairs surrounded a table that had seen better days. It was close enough to Frank that he could see gouges in its top, near where the radio sat. His eyes widened and he gasped. *Those look like fingernail gouges.*

The gasp drew von Haussen's attention.

"Ah, yes. I see you have noticed our table. Some of our patients enter the facility in a less-than-willing manner. Please, pay it no attention. None of our patients are dangerous anymore. The ones that would be considered as such are kept well sedated. "

"What the hell happened to the carpet?" Frank inquired.

Von Haussen laughed, "Ah yes. It seems to be something of a tasty treat to a few of our ward. "

Frank forced a smile. His knees felt weak and his stomach turned. He did NOT want to be here. Psycho-crazy-insane folk scared the hell out of him. They just looked dead and broken. He had argued with Mr. Wainwright, the owner of Wainwright Plumbing, for over an hour about doing a job here. Frank had only been with WP for a few months and was in no position to turn down a job. Mr. Wainwright had made that absolutely clear.

"Mr. Daggets? Mr. Daggets!" von Haussen snapped. "Oh, I'm sorry. I--" Frank started to speak.

"Mr. Daggets, I know a sanitarium is not the most

comfortable place to be, but you must keep your focus. We need these repairs done and my staff's time is very limited. We do not have time to hold your hand. Is that clear? " von Haussen said, obviously irritated.

"My apologies, Mr. von Haussen. Please show me to the areas that need the work," Frank said, flushed with embarrassment.

"This way," von Haussen directed.

Both men and the guard walked down a long cinder block-lined hallway. The walls were painted a putrid green; not a lime color, not an avocado color. Something in-between. The paint clung loosely to the walls. Years of moisture had taken its toll on the paint. Large flakes of the hideous color hung, folded over, off of the walls.

The hall ended at a large steel door. The guard stepped to the front. His keys jingled as he grabbed them. He selected the correct key and inserted it into the lock. The guard gave it a turn and with a metal on metal clang the lock released and von Haussen pushed the door open.

"We are now in the disturbed patient wing of the facility. Most of these patients are here due to some sort of disorder that was too much for their families to deal with. A handful of them are here for crimes against humanity. As I mentioned earlier, you needn't worry about our patients. Those in the violent wards are kept in a constant state of sedation. Should one of the wards bother you, please let a guard or a nurse know. Now, to troubles at hand. Nixon, would you mind? "

The guard, Nixon, stepped forward and again searched through his keys until he found the one he was looking for. He inserted it into the lock and gave it a turn. Again, the familiar metallic clang broke the silence and the door unlocked.

Nothing could have prepared Frank for this.

The smell was atrocious. It assaulted every one of his senses. Every damn one! The foul smell of human shit filled the air. It hung so thick that Frank could taste it.

They stepped inside the small room. Despite the shit smell, Frank's attention immediately went to the woman in the corner of the room.

She sat on a metal bed that was bolted to the wall. A paper-thin mattress lined the bed. She wore white pants and a white shirt. The woman looked to be in her early thirties. She sat staring at Frank. No sound. No movement. *Is she even breathing?* She looked like a mannequin.

3

Just then, the sound of a flushing toilet was heard from somewhere down the corridor. The toilet in the cell began to gurgle.

"Step back, here is goes again," Nixon said, and took his own advice.

Feces spewed from the throat of the toilet. It looked like thick brown toothpaste. Air was also forced through the pipe. That made things even worse. As the air, a horrendous smelling breeze, was forced through the fecal paste, it popped like a bubbling cauldron. Specks of feces shot into the air. Frank watched as Nixon and von Haussen retched.

"The whole--west side--is like this. It is-- Please, just fix it," von Haussen said

Frank nodded and turned back toward the door.

"Jesus Christ!" Frank yelled as he lost his balance on the slippery sludge-covered floor. He fell on his ass directly through the door and landed back in the corridor. "What the fuck is--"

Frank, now on his back, stared up into the doorway. There she stood. The woman from the room, her blank stare locked onto Frank. Again, no movement, no sound. Frank's heart pounded, his eyes wide.

Then blackness.

Frank awoke to von Haussen's voice. "Are you ok? Frank? Can you hear me? "

"What the hell just happened?" Frank interrupted as the memory of the woman's face returned.

"I should have warned you. Sometimes our patients exhibit behaviors that are completely normal for them but not for sane people. Like Claire; she's a sniffer. She smells everything she gets close to. Doesn't talk, doesn't move much, just sniffs," the guard interjected. "We're so used to her and she already knows what we smell like and uh... I was distracted by all the crap. I'm very sorry."

"My god," Frank said, laying his head on the ground. He brought his hands up to his face and wiped the moisture off. *This job is going to be--worse than awful.* Frank wiped his sweaty hands onto his dark blue uniform trousers. Nixon extended his hand. Frank latched on and was pulled to his feet.

"Thanks," Frank said. He brushed the muck off his back and pants.

"You fainted real good there," Nixon said. "You need a few minutes to pull it together?"

"No! I want to get this done as fast as possible. I need to get my tools." Frank said to von Haussen.

"I'll leave you in the care of Mr. Nixon. He will escort you in and out of the main door. You will be provided a key that opens the individual cells, as we do not have the staffing to post someone with you all of the time. I ask that you open only one cell at a time please. We would not want any escapees," von Haussen said.

With that, Frank nodded and together he and Nixon walked back to the doorway that secured the corridor. They passed through and Frank heard the clang of the door being locked.

"I'll be back in just a few minutes," Frank said as he glanced back at Nixon.

Nixon nodded and Frank proceeded to the front door. He grabbed the handle, a cold brass lever, and pushed it down. The wind had picked up significantly since Frank had arrived. It shoved the heavy door into him as he opened it. Once outside it took two hands for Frank to pull it closed.

The rain had died down slightly but the sky was still lit with lightning and cracked with thunder. Anxiously, Frank descended the stairs. His boots splashed into the puddles that soaked the now muddy driveway. Rain splattered his face. He wiped at it furiously with his already wet sleeve. The wind gusted as Frank leaned into the back of his pickup. He lifted the blue tarp that covered his tools and began to look for what he needed.

Shhhh, the wind seemed to speak to Frank. Goosebumps sprang out of his arms. He ignored the noise and continued to rummage for the required tools. *Fraaank,* the wind spoke again. *Behind you, Fraaank.* This was too much for him to ignore. He was flooded with nervous energy.

A gust of wind caught the tarp and whipped it out of the truck bed and over Frank's head.

He panicked and began violently writhing inside the tarp. He fought against the wind. It wrapped the tarp around Frank. He stumbled in a struggle to get the tarp off. Something pushed into him. Through the tarp the wind spoke again. *You will die here, Fraaank.*

Frank ripped at the tarp. He pulled it in one direction and then in the other, fighting to find the edge. Finally, after several more seconds, he found the edge of the tarp. He pulled and pulled until it slipped off his head. Quickly, he looked around for the person that had said those terrifying words to him. He was alone...

As fast as he could, Frank grabbed at the tools. His arms filled with the drain snake, plunger, and a tool box, he made a run for the steps. The tools clanged in their metal container. His boots splashed through the puddles, spraying his pant legs with mud.

He ascended the stairs expeditiously; the wind pushed at his back. With his elbow, he pushed down on the handle as a bolt of lightning illuminated the sky. It was followed shortly by a crack of thunder. He heart pounded in his chest. His elbow slipped off the door handle. The wind's voice returned and whispered to him, *Go inside, Fraaank.*

His elbow caught on the latch as the voice spoke. The wind gusted and shoved the heavy door open. It slammed into the wall from the force. A loud thud filled the air. In a panic Frank's tools crashed onto the hardwood floor. Nixon rushed back into the room from the patient wing.

"You all right, Frank? "Nixon asked, with a concerned look on his face. "You are white as a sheet."

"Yeah, I'm fine. I'm just cold and wet," Frank lied.

"Shut that door would ya? I don't want to catch my death in here. "

"Yeah. Sorry, damn wind is vicious," Frank said.

"Sure is," Nixon replied. "Grab your tools; I'll let you in the wing again before I head to lunch."

Frank picked up his tools and walked to where Nixon was standing.

"Who is replacing you while you go to lunch?" he inquired.

"We ain't got that many guards, so I just go to lunch and come back. It's only an hour or so. The nurses go at the same time so as they ain't gotta worry 'bout bein' let in and out," Nixon said matter-of-factly.

"Wait. Let me get this straight. You are going to lock me in there with a bunch of psychos? ALONE? You can't do that. What if I need to get out? What if something happens and I need help?" Frank pleaded.

"Listen Frank, they ain't gonna do nothin' and you'll be fine. The nurses just finished their rounds and medicated the ones who need it. It's gonna be quiet as a church in there. It's nap time," Nixon said with a smile.

They walked back down the hall to the door at the entrance to the disturbed patient wing. Nixon fumbled with his keys, unlocked and opened the door. Frank stepped in and set his tools down by the first door on the west side of the hallway. Frank, still holding his keys, located the one that opens the patient doors and spun it off the key-ring.

"Here ya go. 'Member, only one door at a time. Don't want a hall full of coo-coos," Nixon laughed and handed Frank the key.

He took it and slid it in his pocket. Nixon backed out of the corridor and fingered through his keys. Frank heard the clang again and said his goodbye to Nixon.

"See ya in an hour," Nixon said.

Nixon's footsteps faded as he walked away, leaving Frank cold, wet, and alone. He leaned back against the steel door next to where he set his tools. *You'll be fine. It's not that bad. Nothing bad can happen to you in here. Just do your job.*

Thinking that all is fine and well–in the presence of the sun–on a well-lit day. But it's hard to swallow your own bullshit in a hall of crazy people, where the lights are barely lit, and sounds of moaning and whispering filled the air. *I hate this fucking job! And I hate these fucking psychos!*

He knelt and opened his tool box, then selected a handful of tools he thought he may need. He also secured the snake and the plunger. This was going to be messy. He slipped his hand into the pocket, removed the key, and inserted it in the lock. Frank took a deep breath and gave it a turn. Clang. The door opened.

Frank took a moment to evaluate the room before entering. The foul smell was significantly less in this room. *It must be past the blockage.* There was no overflowing mountain of fecal paste. That was a relief. He decided that this was a good room to start in since he wouldn't have to lie in any shit.

Frank anxiously entered the room and scanned for the patient that lived there. He gave it a once over but saw no patient. He looked again, more frantically. No one was in the room but him, it appeared.

This room was set up exactly like the last. The metal bed against the far-left wall. The toilet bolted to the wall near the door. And the cabinet in the far-right corner. Frank walked in and set his tools down. He was relieved that he started in this room. There was a distinct possibility that he may not have to be in an occupied cell. If he could manage to snake and plunge out whatever the clog was then maybe, just maybe--

Frank reached behind the toilet and found the water shut- off and twisted it. It squeaked closed. Frank gave the toilet a flush in hopes that the water would clear out of the bowl. It partially worked. He laughed to himself as he heard a toilet gurgle down the corridor and imagined the flow of shit pouring out of the toilet.

This was the best it was going to get so he located the half inch wrench and went to work loosening the bolts. Several minutes later the nuts were off the bolts and all there was to do was pull the toilet up. Frank knelt and grabbed onto the bowl. He pulled. The bolts creaked as the bowl slid off. A small trickle of water leaked out of the back of the toilet. *That wasn't so bad.*

Frank grabbed the snake. It was nothing more than a round metal cable that you pushed into the drain. On one end it had an auger bit and on the other there was a handle with a crank on it. As you turned the crank, the auger spun, chewing away at the blockage. This was usually the most effective method of clearing a drain.

He pushed the snake into the drain. This particular one had fifty feet of cable that you could feed in. Frank fed the line in and felt the pipe curve. There was no blockage yet, so he continued to push. Eighteen or so feet in, the snake stopped. He gave it a push. *Nothing. This must be the blockage.* Frank began to crank the auger.

Outside the thunder continued. It was much louder that it had been. He could hear it inside the building now and it sounded as loud as it had been when he was standing outside. Thunder cracked again. Frank could hear movement down the corridor. *They must be scared.* He continued to crank the auger.

Whatever this is, it is one hell of a block. He cranked the auger faster and put more pressure on the cable. More thunder cracked. The walls rumbled from the concussion. A blood curdling scream pierced the air. Moans increased as the screams intensified. The patients began banging on the doors. Nonsensical chatter filled the air. Frank could occasionally make out words.

One patient relatively close was screaming and intermittently yelling, "They're raping me! They're raping me! Jesus' baby is dead! I have the devil's baby in me now!"

Frank stood, his body full of nervous energy. He stepped into the hall and looked down the corridor. It was empty. He listened closely to the woman rambling.

"Fuck me with your devil cock!

I'll have your demon seed!

Now put your dick inside of me and we'll begin to breed!" she intoned.

"Jesus Christ," Frank whispered to himself. *This place is crazy.* Frank had heard enough and walked back into the room and knelt next to the toilet. He grabbed the snake and cranked. The blockage dislodged. There was now a pushing force on the end of the snake. *It must be water backup.*

Frank began to re-spool the snake. Again, thunder cracked. There was a bang at the end of the corridor. Frank jumped at the noise. He clamped the snake to the side of the drain and stood. *What the fuck is that?* The banging echoed down the hall again. He walked to the hall. Thunder cracks continued to rumble against the walls. The lights flickered.

"Holy fuck... This is not ok," he said. He glanced at his watch. It had only been twenty minutes since Nixon had left for lunch. The lights flickered again as the banging continued. He slowly crept down the hall toward its source. His arms filled with goose bumps. From the cell next to him a blood curdling scream blasted into his ears. He jumped and ran several cells further down the hall toward the banging.

Half a minute later he found himself standing in front of the cell with the pounding. On the doors there were circular portholes with metal covers. Frank had seen one of the nurses using one when he first arrived. He reached for the cover and slid it to the left. The banging stopped. Curious he leaned forward and peered in.

Nothing.

The room looked empty. He pressed his face into the glass peephole.

Nothing.

Frank slid his hand into his pocket and felt for the key. *Shit, it's in the other cell.* He was glad that he didn't see anything inside the cell and that he didn't have the key. *These people are fucking terrifying. What the hell was I thinking?*

He hastily returned back to the first cell. His snake was lying on the ground, completely out of the pipe when he entered the room. *What the fuck? Must have been some kind of pressure in there, to push out six feet of snake.* Frank grabbed the snake and fed it back into the pipe. Exactly at the same point, he ran into the blockage again. This perplexed Frank. *How did the pressure blow out my snake but not the block?*

He reluctantly began to crank the auger again. The blockage moved and he began to pull out the block once more. With about two feet of snake left in the pipe, the block got caught. *Damn, almost there.* He cranked the auger. The clog moved. He pulled the snake free of the pipe just as the thunder cracked again.

This time the lights went out. Water and several solid, wet objects flew from the pipe, striking Frank mid-chest. He emitted a guttural howl and scrambled to wipe off whatever struck him. He stood, knees shaking. A wail broke into the silent darkness. Frank screamed again.

"Fuck!"

The banging resumed down the hall. Thunder roared in the atmosphere. Frank heard something move in the room behind him. He sprang to his feet. He stuck his arms out and searched for the doorway. He had a flashlight in his tool box. He had to get it.

Another noise, a creak, came from directly behind him. "Who's there?" Frank yelled.

Footsteps padded across the floor inside the room. Frank felt a quick breeze of air rush past him.

In a frenzy, Frank grabbed the wall and pushed his way to the doorway. He felt the steel door and rushed into the corridor, slamming it shut behind him. Quickly, he dropped to the floor and searched for his toolbox. He found it and removed the top tray, spilling its contents onto the floor. Ratchets and wrenches clanged against the cement.

There, at the bottom of the toolbox, Frank's hand found it. The familiar cylindrical shape of his flashlight. He grabbed it tightly with two hands. His thumb searched for the switch. He flicked it.

"AGH!!!!AGH! AGH!" filled the air. Frank turned the flashlight toward the sounds.

"OH FUCK!" he yelled. There, in his beam of light, stood a pale-skinned woman with ratty brown hair. She was dressed in a white and blue nightgown and was clutching her hair, pulling it out from her scalp.

She screamed again, pulling out more gnarled hair from her scalp, "Wha Wha! Rhoa!"

She continued to scream and pull her hair out, but now she began to walk toward him.

"Get back!" Frank yelled.

He grabbed the metal tool tray from the floor and swung it at the woman as she advanced. Her face was sunken in like starving Ethiopian's.

Frank shook as he swung the tray at her but missed. She wouldn't stop. Finally close enough, Frank took another swing. This time it connected. The tray made a sickening thwack as it collided with her head. Immediately Frank saw a gash open in her forehead. It wasn't enough to put her down though. It was merely a glancing blow.

Another scream pierced the air. She extended her hair-filled hands out at him, then lunged. He swung the tray and it connected. Firmly. The woman fell to the floor. Frank stood and swung the tray at her head. He struck her over and over until she stopped moving.

He ran to the door at the end of the corridor. The door where he had last seen Nixon. He grabbed the handle and shook it, all the while he was yelling.

"Let me out! Help! I need out! They are going to fucking kill me!"

His eyes blurred with tears. He felt them rolling down his cheeks. No one came.

They could not hear his screams. *What am I going to do? Oh, God. Oh, God. Oh, God.* He shook the door again, pulling as hard as he could. He pushed. And kicked. And shoved. And punched, until his sobs overcame him, and he slunk to the floor.

He sat with his back against the steel door. His flashlight shined on the feet of the woman he had just clubbed with a tool tray. Other patients could be heard milling about, but each was locked in their room. *Where did she come from? How?*

Several minutes passed as he sat there sobbing. Frank checked his watch. *Fifteen more minutes until Nixon returns. Then he can get me the fuck out of here!* The woman's feet twitched in the light. He couldn't sit in the hall and watch this for fifteen minutes. *What if she woke up?* He grabbed the flashlight and stood. Overwhelmed with fear, he bolted into the now open cell.

Frank entered the cell. The room's cabinet was illuminated by the thin beam of light. The doors were now open. There seemed plenty of room for a small woman to fit in there. Frank's focus locked on the cabinet. She must have been in there the whole time. He noticed some writing on the back-interior wall of the cabinet. Slowly, he stepped closer to inspect the words.

"Jesus Christ," Frank murmured quietly.

Scratched into the back wall of the cabinet was a single word. HELP! He inspected it closer. It looked to have been scratched into the paint by fingernails. Frank stepped closer and examined it further. Small droplets of wet blood were smeared throughout the scratched surface. He knelt and reached forward to touch a small white object, a fingernail that protruded from the scratches. A thunder clap broke through the darkness.

The patients began to scream again. Frank jumped at the sudden noise. He jumped and struck his head. His foot slipped on the wet floor. His body struck the cement floor with a thud. His head followed suit and cracked against the floor. Frank's vision flashed white momentarily. The flashlight flew from his hand. He grabbed at the back of his head with both hands and winced in pain.

Frank lay motionless on the floor. He stayed like this until he regained his vision. He opened his eyes. His vision still blurred. Light illuminated the area in front of his face. *The flashlight must be just above my head.* He reached for it. His hand grasped onto an object. It was wet and softer than he expected. He pulled it into the beam of light. His eyes strained to focus. As they did, something horrific appeared.

A semi-rotted rat face glared back at him. One eye was popped out of its skull and hung on by a meaty thread. Frank lost it. His body began to convulse. He turned his head and spewed

vomit. It splashed onto the floor. He threw the rat carcass and pushed himself up off the floor. Tears filled his eyes. He reached for the flashlight.

As he did, he saw them. Seven...eight... No! Ten! Ten more rat bodies lay strewn on the floor. All were in various stages of decay. Frank spewed more vomit. More tears ran down his face. He grabbed his flashlight and ran out the door. He shined it at the exit door. Still no Nixon.

Then he heard it.

The sound came from the floor next to him. Where he had left the twitching girl. He directed his beam of light at the spot. Now, where there had been only one, there were two. A female form dressed in white pants and a white shirt sat hunched over the still quivering body.

Frank froze.

Where had she come from? This second woman moved her head

around the neck area of the girl lying on the floor. Frank stared as she moved.

He cried out, pleading, "What are you doing? Please... Stop!"

His body quaked as she turned her head toward him. They locked eyes. Blood covered her nose and mouth. It was the sniffer! He stared at Frank. He stared back. Neither moved.

A familiar clang sounded from behind Frank. The door opened.

"Frank? You in here?" Nixon yelled.

Frank yelled incoherently, "Ugh! I gotta-- Fuh! Agh!"

He ran past Nixon, and nearly knocked him down. He ran down the hall toward the entrance. Frank heard footsteps behind him. He heard thunder crashing above him. He heard his heart pounding. He heard these things until he heard them no more. His brain rang and filled his ears with a buzzing sound. Frank grasped the handle to the exit door. He slammed his shoulder into it as he gave the handle a turn.

His body bounced off the door and he fell to the ground. He scrambled. Unable to get to his feet Frank grabbed the handle while still on his hands and knees. A gust of wind shoved the door open. He looked outside.

The sky flashed with near-continuous lightning. His ears filled only with buzzing. It felt like he was trapped in a silent picture. Frank crawled outside onto the stoop. He rolled down the steps, still unable to stand. He crawled through puddles in the drive while he made his way to his truck.

Trapped in the buzzing, Frank reached for the truck's door handle. Still on his hands and knees, he grabbed hold. He pushed the wet, chrome button in. The door opened slightly, the wind pushing against it. Frank whipped it open further and grabbed the steering wheel.

He hoisted himself in the truck. He hastily inserted and turned the key. The gauges on the dash illuminated. Frank grabbed the shifter and yanked it into drive. He mashed the pedal to the floor. The truck lurched forward, causing the driver's door to slam shut.

Sprays of dirt and mud flew into the air behind the speeding vehicle. Frank glanced into the rear-view mirror. He saw several people standing outside the Sanitarium. He could only make out Nixon and von Haussen.

His eyes went back to the road. The accelerator was still slammed to the floor. Trees whipped by the windows as the truck sped forward. Frank cried. His tears ran down his face and dripped onto his muddy shirt. *I knew I shouldn't have gone there. Fucking psychos--*

He wiped his eyes. Standing in the road, right in front of his truck, was a woman. She was soaked with rain. What remaining hair she had was matted to her face. It was the woman he had struck with the tool tray!

"No!" Frank screamed.

He grabbed the wheel with both hands and yanked it to the left. The truck lurched and narrowly missed the woman. He tried to correct the steering, but the speed was too much. The truck leapt from the road into the woods.

Frank bounced around inside the cab until there was only blackness.

Frank woke up some time later. A dim yellow light glowed above his head. Von Haussen stood above him looking down.

A nurse stepped in. A needle pricked into Frank's shoulder.

"It's nap time, Frank. We gotta go to lunch. Try not to cause any trouble this time, eh? "he heard Nixon say.

"Welcome to Laurel Mountain, Mr. Daggets," von Haussen said with a crooked smile. "Enjoy your new home."

BELLUM SACRUM

I wish you would just die already! You are a lazy, backstabbing piece of shit!" Mark screamed at his co-worker. His face was flushed with excitement. He was finally getting all his pent-up anger out. It had been building for so long and now was blasting out, unencumbered, uncensored, and in front of all his peers.

It was wonderful!

Faces, mostly blurred, filled Mark Thomas's peripheral vision. Even obscured as they were, he could see all of the gaping jaws. It looked like twenty trout staring at him. He continued to scream obscenities at Lin Alvonellos, the office fuck-up. Vile words spewed out of his mouth. Spittle splashed on Lin's face, splattered on the walls and desk as he unloaded his fury.

Lin just stood there, stupefied, as if he was too dumb to comprehend the hate-filled rant. Mark watched as he stepped back while the barrage impacted. He watched Lin's face change from simple and ignorant to confused and pained.

Lin rubbed his left arm and begin to scratch—no, more like claw at —the side of his neck. Red marks appeared on his irritated skin as Lin feverishly raked, but nothing was going to stop Mark. He had waited too long for this very moment; Lin had done far too much stupid shit. This was his time to shine.

"You are a stupid fuck! How can anyone be so dumb? Don't just stand there, say something! I want you dead!" Mark yelled.

All that Lin could muster was the same stupid thing he always said. "Oh, good." It didn't matter if you said your granny just died, it was only thing Lin ever sputtered.

And it was the last thing he ever sputtered. Without another word, Lin grabbed his chest, made a stupid face, and dropped dead.

Right there in front of the whole office. Just dropped dead.

It was the first time Mark had ever killed someone, and he had only used his words. He thought for sure they were going to suspend and fire him on the spot. Hell, the Human Resources bitch, "Tasty" Carlson, just stood there slowly smothering to death in her epic fat rolls, not saying a word.

It never happened though. Mark just returned to his cubicle and went back to watching YouTube videos. Tasty stopped eating her Ho Hos long enough to call 911. Mark could hear the bitch screaming, "He's dead, ohhh, he's dead—"

Mark just rolled his eyes and put his headphones in. Sometime later, the ambulance arrived and carted Lin off. Mark didn't even bother to look up from his screen. It was a good day.

Before long, the police were asking him to fill out a statement on what had happened.

Mark simply told them, "No, thank you," and returned to YouTube until the work day was over. He found that each interaction filled him with a sense of joy and accomplishment. Each time he said something out of the ordinary, he felt titillated. Soon enough, five o'clock arrived and without a word, not even so much as a glance at the other employees, he walked out and went home.

THE next morning Mark awoke to the piercing beep-beep-beep of his alarm clock. His brain began whirring awake. He immediately recalled yesterday's events, cracking a smile as they replayed in his head. *I can't believe he just died. I would have yelled at him far sooner if I thought that would have happened.*

He lay there, snug and self-satisfied in his bed for a few more minutes before deciding to get up. He sprang from his bed, filled with exhilaration. He had to do something to rid himself of some of this energy, so he shed his boxers and did what every twenty-five-year-old does.

Masturbation seemed to have lost its ability to calm him, however. He was still so full of energy. Sure, he'd been energetic before, but never like this. It was like a dozen A.D.D. kids off their meds were bouncing around in his brain. *Jesus fuck, man...*

Mark hopped in the shower and raced through washing. He needed to do something to get rid of this energy. He felt out of control and had to rein it in. *What can I do? What will make me feel better? A run maybe?*

He bounded out of the shower and grabbed his socks and shoes. He sat on the couch still dripping wet after forgetting to dry himself. Socks on. Shoes on. Laces tied. He was out the door and halfway down the block.

Run, run, running... *Gotta go faster. Can't stop running.* His body coursed with his life-blood. He slowed and looked at his smartwatch to check his pulse. Fifty-five beats per minute. *How could that be? I was practically sprinting.*

He took another look at the heart rate monitor. Fifty-four, fifty-three, fifty-two... the countdown continued. He bolted into a sprint again. His mind raced as his heart barely puttered along. He checked again. The rate was locked at forty-eight.

He picked up the pace. No change. He ran full out, as fast as his body would move. No change. *What the fuck!*

He stopped, expecting to be panting after sprinting so hard. He was barely breathing faster than when he slept. Fourteen times a minute is what he counted. Shit, Tasty Carlson breathed that much just thinking about a Snickers.

Honk! A car horn blared.

"What the fuck are you doing? Get some clothes on, you pervert!" the man yelled from the car.

What? Mark looked down. He was horrified at what he saw. His giblets hung out in the open for everyone to see. His pasty white skin glowed like snow on a sunny day. *I forgot clothes. I'm naked. I'm naked,* he paused, looking around, *in the middle of downtown.*

"Get out of the road, faggot! No one wants to see your tiny dick-lett!" a kid yelled out the window of an approaching school bus. The bus's brakes squealed as it came to a stop at the light.

This can't be happening. It must be a dream. He felt his face flush with embarrassment.

"Ha! Look at his tiny dick!" a ginger teen yelled, pointing out the window.

Before he knew it, Mark's mouth was open and spewing words: "It's not tiny, you motherfuckers!"

"Why are you naked? What a freak!" the ginger replied.

"I'm gonna come up there and light you on fire, you little fucker!" Mark yelled.

"With what? You gonna rub your tiny dick 'til it shoots sparks?" The ginger laughed. The whole bus laughed as Mark scanned the windows. Each one had at least two faces pressed against their panes. Some even had three.

Mark balled his fists. He could feel the rage building inside him. *Who do they think they are? I'm not one you want to fuck with. I killed someone yesterday, just by yelling at them!*

Mark opened his mouth to yell again but all that escaped was a tiny squeak, like when his voice cracked as a pubescent boy. That was all the kids needed. They unleashed a barrage of names and puberty jokes.

One kid even had the audacity to scream, "I think he just grew a pube!"

"I have lots of pubes. I just shave them!" Mark yelled.

"That way they don't stick in your mommy's teeth!" the ginger yelled.

"You're fucking dead, you little bitch," Mark mumbled.

His head filled with thoughts of blowing up the school bus. He envisioned the little ginger brat melting into a pile of human goo. He imagined the rest of the bus bursting into flames.

Mark's ears were ringing now, filled with a tinnitus-like hum. He stuck his arms out in front of himself toward the bus. He pretended to be choking the kids. *Those smart-ass little shits. What did they know, anyways?*

He imagined the vinyl seats catching fire as the children frantically climbed over them to get off the bus and put out the fires that engulfed them. Mark could see the yellow paint charring to black. He could smell the rubber of the tires burning.

A car horn sounded to his left. A long, deep, irritating honk. Mark pointed his left hand at that car as if telling the driver that the honking had to stop.

His brain pulsed with the sounds. Another horn blasted from the offending car. Mark would do anything to make it stop. He thought of a tree falling. Crashing onto the car, crushing it, smashing the driver into a thick red mush. He imagined the bus catching the fallen tree limbs ablaze.

This would, of course, catch the car on fire, effectively melting its cheap polyester foam-filled seats into nothingness. The hum in his ears was drowning out the world around him.

He was sure any minute now the police would be arriving to take his naked self into custody. But that didn't happen. Mark just stood there, cowering behind his arms, pretending the horrible things he was thinking were really happening. He could feel his body shaking. He drew his hands in close to his face and squatted down.

Eventually the hum dimmed and was replaced by the sound of his racing heart. It was pounding so fast he couldn't even count the beats. Mark fell into the fetal position. He could feel the cement underneath his body as he settled onto the porous surface. It wasn't cool like he expected it to be. It was warm, very warm in fact. And what was that smell...?

Ignoring the heat for a moment, Mark peeked at his heart rate sensor. Three-hundred-two beats per minute. Was he having a heart attack? A stroke? Was that why the cement felt so warm? That would explain the humming in his ears too.

Afraid this might be the last time he would see the world, he convinced himself to open his eyes.

"Oh, my god—"

The school bus *was* on fire. The kids moved frantically inside, crawling over seats attempting to escape. The fire was so hot the glass windows began to warp, and the paint began to blister. The hum that had once blocked Mark from hearing anything had dissipated, and his ears now filled with the screams of flaming children.

Mark sat up. This was unbelievable. This is exactly what he had imagined. And now it was happening right in front of him. *But how?* A piercing scream belted from his left. The car, the one that had been honking at him, was fully engulfed as well. Mark could see the driver was also ablaze. A tree had fallen on top of the car and onto the bus, and once the diesel tank had flamed up, the fire had transferred to the car.

Mark sat, nude, and in awe, as the world around him burned.

END credits rolled on whatever television movie had been playing. Mark sat on his couch, beer in hand, staring blankly at the screen. He was exhausted from the morning's events. He'd never felt so powerful before.

What was that? Was that really me that caused that? If so... I'm practically invincible. Invincible and exhausted. Maybe I can try a little more after a quick nap.

Mark slumped over onto the nearby pillow. He didn't really want to sleep on the couch, but he was too tired to move to his bed.

He awoke to pounding at his front door. Whispers drifted lightly across the air, tickling his ears.

"Take your positions. Wait for my command, then move in.

Sound off when you are in position," a voice whispered. Mark immediately put it together; the police were outside his house and about to pay him a little visit.

His stomach churned with panic; it felt almost like butterflies on steroids. He was starting to enjoy this feeling. It made him feel so alive! The familiar feeling of his beating heart returned. Much like a sports car, it idled quietly but, like a well- tuned machine, at the right moment, it throttled up. This was that moment.

"Mark Thomas, this is the police. You have ten seconds to come out with your hands in the air!" the voice boomed.

His heart revved up. Vroom, vroom. He looked at his wrist and tapped the smartwatch navigating to the heart-rate sensor. Vroom, vroom! Ninety, one hundred, one-fifty. The countdown began outside.

"Ten!"

He began to shake. The butterflies in his stomach turned to angry dragons. The fire in him grew.

His worked his hands in and out of fists, rubbing the clenched one before punching it into the other with a *crack!* Switching hands. Another *crack!* Seconds passed. The hum returned to his ears.

"Five!" the voice boomed from outside.

This was it. Five seconds from now, one of two things were going to happen. Either he would be dead or they would be. One way or another, only one side would walk away.

"Three!"

Mark began sweating heavily. No time to run. Not that he wanted to. "Two!"

"Go fuck yourselves!" he yelled at the top of his lungs. "One!"

There was an enormous thud at the wooden front door. It was followed quickly by two more. Thud. Thud. Then, with one last blow, the door exploded into hundreds of splinters.

Police charged into the house. Half a dozen entered from the front, a few through the windows, and even more from the rear. All for him. All for someone that had done nothing. Nothing tangible anyway.

Mark stood still in his living room, hands deep in his pants pockets. Thump-thump, thump-thump.

"Can I help you officers?" Mark asked. Thump-thump- thump. Thump-thump-thump.

"Hands in the air! Now!" the officers yelled.

"As you wish," he replied. Thump-thump-thump-thump-thump-thump—

Mark's hands shot into the air. The motion was so fast, it spooked one of the officers, a young kid who look to be in his twenties. Gunfire burst into the air. Rifles and pistols alike fired. Pop, pop, pop.

In just a matter of seconds, hundreds of rounds flew directly at Mark. The rounds impacted with his skin, instantly turning to molten metal. The glowing hot liquid splashed onto the floor, igniting the carpet.

The room filled with smoke and gunpowder from the discharging firearms. The officers stepped closer, still unleashing a barrage of rounds at him.

Liquid metal splashed back onto their skin or clothing, burning holes wherever it landed. Screams of pain joined the gunfire. Some of the men dropped to their knees, trying to wipe the molten liquid off.

Mark could see the twenty-something officer that started the battle. His face had several holes in it and blood was pouring out of the spot where his tongue used to be. It looked like the metal just ate it away.

He stared at the officer, smiling. *This is the coolest thing ever! I can do whatever the fuck I want! Even bullets can't stop me.* The hum in his ears had lessened now and was replaced by the ever-growing screams and gurgles.

He reached out to the young man kneeling in front of him. A fluid-filled gasp followed by a deeply drowned out: "Help me" poured from the man.

"Help? Is that what you want?" Mark asked.

The man shook his head in the affirmative.

"Very well."

Mark jerked the pistol free from the officer's holster and pointed it at his injured forehead. The youth shook with fear at the sight. Mark saw his pants darken as he pissed himself like a baby.

"Don't be afraid. I won't shoot you," Mark said, dropping the Glock's magazine. One by one, he flicked the rounds out of the magazine and into his hand. Relief filled the officer's face.

Once empty, Mark cupped his hands together over the ammunition. Brief fizzles of the rounds going off could be heard. *This is neat. It doesn't even hurt.* Mark peeked into his hands.

"As you requested, my boy!" Mark plunged the first two fingers into the molten metal. Before the boy know what was happening, Mark, using his fingers, splashed the liquid down, from his forehead to his upper lip. A second horizontal splash and a masterful upside-down cross was melting through his face and head.

Mark took the remaining liquid and slapped the next police officer across the face. He began laughing at the sight of death. One after the other, Mark melted whatever metal he could touch, and flung, plunged, or punched it into the nearest person.

The pungent aroma of sulfur and burning flesh was rampant throughout the house. Less than three minutes after police started this mess, it was over. His heart slowed down and a fatigue set in. He was not nearly as tired this time. No nap would be necessary. Just a brief rest. Mark sat on the couch in the burning living room.

Flames raged and had engulfed most of the dining room and kitchen. It wouldn't be long now until the rest of the house joined in the festivities. He could see the remains of people turning into white ash and floating up into the air.

Mark sat in awe of his work. *This all seems like a dream.* He hoped it wasn't. *This shit is way too cool to be a dream.*

Just then he heard sirens. *Firetrucks. I better go.* Mark stood and immediately collapsed onto the floor. His consciousness escaped him.

Mark awoke, not sure where he was or what was happening. A man in a black suit approached. "Hi, Mark. It's been a long time," he said in a thick southern drawl.

"Who the fuck are you?" Mark asked.

"Mark. Mark. Mark. My dear boy. Let's dispatch with the unpleasantries, shall we?"

"What's going on?"

"My boy, the hour is near. There are a few things that need explaining. First off: Your mouth stays shut. Another word out of it and I'll seal it. Understand?"

Mark started to speak, then nodded.

The man in black stared at him. "Secondly: I don't care what you believe in, who you believe in, or even why you believe in them. Forget what you know. You don't know shit, my boy! Is that clear enough for you?"

"Okay. But who—"

"Uh uh. What did I say about talking? We'll get there. Just join me on the ride."

With that, the room went black.

The light slowly returned, and Mark found himself seated in an old wooden chair. Space and time moved around him as the man waved his arms.

"My boy... Welcome to 1988. That Godawful music blaring on the television is *Sister Christian* by Night Ranger. That whore in the corner is none other than your mother. And that scumbag meth-head beating her... Well, that's dear old Dad."

Mark began to recognize the area as the blur of motion faded. It was his Granny's basement. He had spent a lot of time here when he was younger. After his dad left.

"How is this possible? How am I here? What are you?" Mark interjected.

"Shhh. Relax." Mark noticed a letter on the nearby table and retrieved it. A foreclosure notice. While he read the letter, he'd almost forgotten that his father had been beating the shit out of his mother. A brief scream served as a reminder.

"I told you to shut up, you stupid cunt!" his father yelled. "Jack, stop! Please. I'll do whatever you want."

"You'll do whatever I want *and* get the rest of this whoopin', understand?"

"Plea—" His mom was cut off by a fist to the jaw.

"I had no idea he beat her like this. I never even met the guy. He just up and left one day."

It was painful for Mark to watch. Blood poured from his mother's mouth. Drips and splashes coated the floor under her. There was even a solitary tooth lying in a small pool of red liquid.

"Make it stop. I can't watch any more of this," Mark said.

"Oh? A little while ago you lit a bus full of kids on fire, and *now* you have an issue with violence? Ah, well, the world is full of contradictions and double standards. I don't think I'll ever understand it. That's part of the beauty, though. The unpredictability of humanity. It makes things so much more interesting."

Mark listened to the man but focused his attention on his mother. He hated seeing her taking a beating. Hated seeing the pain in her face. He wanted, with everything in his soul, to help her. But he knew he couldn't. This was the past and there was no way to change the past.

"Pay attention, Marky, my boy... It's about to get *good*."

He watched as his father pulled a small silver revolver from his waistband. It had been hiding in his blue jeans under his white tank-top. He pointed it at his mother. Right at her bleeding, sad little face.

She sobbed uncontrollably, pleading with the man. "No! Please, don't hurt me. Please. I have to tell you something. John, I have to tell you! I'm pregnant!" she screamed.

His father momentarily froze, revolver still pointed at her. No words left his mouth. No change in expression. Just the look of fear, rage, and murderous intent that had been there all along.

John pulled back on the trigger. Mark could see the hammer begin to inch back. He couldn't watch this. He wanted with everything in his soul to run to her and save her.

The revolver's hammer crept back. Upon reaching its apex, it slammed forward. But there was no gun shot. No bang, no click, just a soft thump as the hammer slammed into the finger of the man in black. The room froze like someone pressed pause. Mark sat awestruck as he watched the replay of the man in black stop the pistol from going off. He was bewildered.

How could the man be sitting next to him and be in the past? How could any of this be happening? Let's not pull at that thread, shall we?

The man in front of him spoke: "Hello, my dear. Looks like you are having a bad day."

"Who the hell are you?"

"You're a spitting image of her," the man in black beside Mark said.

Mark didn't even look away as the man continued to speak to his mother.

"I bet you are tired of the beatings. The abuse. The impending death. It's pretty terrifying, isn't it?"

"Yeah. You think, genius?" she retorted.

"I'm sorry to have bothered you; it's clear you don't want me here. I'll just pull my finger out and let this miserable existence of yours come to an end."

"No! Wait! I don't want to die. I'm pregnant. I want my child to live. I want him to grow up. I don't want to die! Please!" she begged.

"I would be happy to help, ma'am. But I need a little favor from you," he said.

"Anything! I don't have much money. I don't have fancy things. I just want my baby boy!"

"So do I," he said. "So do I. One day, I will come calling for him. When that time comes, I can't afford for him to say no. I need you to give him to me. Not his physical body so much as— his soul.

"You see, I am in the business of collecting things. It's very important that I collect your son. You may have him until you die. That should suffice, yes?"

"What will you do with him?"

"My intentions are not for you to worry about. I assure you he'll never be harmed. I will even get rid of this monster of a man for you. What do you say?"

"I don't want to get in trouble for killing him. I can't lose my boy. How can you help?"

"Don't worry. I just need your commitment. It's as simple as that. And all your worry goes away. You can spend the rest of your days with your bouncing baby boy. That is what you want, isn't it?"

"Yes. Okay. I'll do it. I'll take your help."

"Excellent choice, my dear. One, I assure you, you'll not regret."

With that, the man pulled a folded piece of parchment from his jacket pocket and opened it. On it, in a language Mark had never seen, were words illegible to him.

"All I need is a signature here," the man said, pointing to an X next to a line on the page. He removed a pen tipped with a serpent head from his pocket. The woman reached for it but he jerked it away.

"Not so fast. This signature needs to be done in a very special way."

Mark saw his mother open her mouth, but before any words left it, the man plunged the pen into her stomach. She gasped in pain as it dug deeper. Not only into her, but into her unborn child.

"It needs to be signed in blood from *his* heart."

With a final thrust, the pen plunged into the baby's heart. Mark's heart. It made him uncomfortable the way the man said the word "his," like it was important.

He watched as the pen was pulled from her belly. Blood coated its outside but quickly drained into the pen. The wound where the pen had pierce her faded away.

The man handed her the pen. "Sign, and all this ends now." He gestured to John and his gun.

She did. Bright red blood flowed behind the tip of the pen. Each loop and line drained more of the fluid. Once finished, the man stood and in the blink of an eye, was gone. Her murderous boyfriend also vanished.

Mark watched her search the room for any sign of either man. There was no trace of them, like they'd never existed.

Again, his vision blurred as the man in black brought Mark back to reality.

"Well, my boy, what do you think? You ready to finish what dear 'ol mom started?"

"Did—Did I just watch my mom sign my soul over to the devil? Jesus fucking Christ... Are you the devil?"

"You better believe it, sonny boy. Lucifer, Beelzebub, the Boogie Man. Call me whatever you want. Just remember, you and your newfound power belong to me."

"What do you want from me? Why me?" Mark asked, scratching his head and desperately trying to put it all together. "Are you trying to start a war? The Apocalypse?"

"Mark, Mark, Mark." The war is already over. Humanity lost. Shit, they lost the day your momma signed that contract."

"What? How?" Mark asked perplexed. "What does any of this have to do with me? Or my mom? Why us?"

"You, Mark. Only you. You were chosen by Him. By God himself to bear the soul of Jesus Christ. The old fucker thought He could get one over on me. Thought He could sneak the Second Coming in, right under my nose.

"He wasn't good enough. I have spies everywhere. Your Granny was one of my informants. It was sad to lose her. Did you know she killed a few people for me? Tough lady, your Granny."

"I don't believe a word out of your lying mouth! My Granny would never help the Devil!" Mark felt a tear roll down his cheek. Just the thought of his grandmother, her smiling face, gray hair, and wrinkles... helping the great evil? *No way!*

"Mark. You are missing the point. It doesn't matter what you think. You are going to do *exactly* what I tell you to do. You don't have a choice. You *can't* say no. I own your soul, control it. You are the bringer of the End Times. The Apocalypse IS HERE!"

Mark stood, determined to leave. There is no way any of this could be true... Could it? Mark felt anger fill him. He began to build with rage at the thought of the Devil touching his family. Making them kill. Stealing his future.

Could I really have been the Second Coming? Jesus reincarnated? There is no reason I can't be. I went to church, studied the Bible. I certainly can withstand the evil that is after me... Right?

"That's your big plan, Mark? Say no to evil? Do I look like a joint? It isn't like the D.A.R.E. program, Marky. You can't just say no. I can feel everything you feel. Hear everything you hear. And the best part is, it's a two-way link.

"Do you feel that rage inside you? That fire? That's me. I'm pushing my power into you. The end is near, my boy! Very near.

You have two choices. You can either do what I say and let me do what I have to do. And if you chose that route, I will remove your conscious, your awareness, your humanity.

"Or you can try and fight me, albeit unsuccessfully, and I'll leave all of you in that little brain of yours. You'll get to watch yourself destroy humanity. All of humanity. Every creature on earth, in fact. How does that sound?"

I don't want to kill anyone. I don't want any of this. I just want to go back to normal. Back to the way it was before I hurt people. I—

"Time's up, Marky. I need His soul and your body to get this done. What'll it be? Shall we wreck this place together?"

His conscience wouldn't let him willingly destroy everything he knows and loves. Everyone he knows and loves. "Fuck you! I won't let you use me!"

"There's the fire! Let it out Mark! Let it mingle with the rage coursing through your veins. You made the right choice, by the way. You'll enjoy what you are about to do."

His head raged with the searing pain of guilt. Regret flooded his soul. He wished now that he'd chosen wisely instead of acting so rashly.

His body was controlled by the Devil but his mind, that was all his. And he had a front row seat to the ruin. Earthquakes shook the city to rubble. Volcanoes shot forth from the earth, spewing their magmatic discharge into the air, covering everything close to them.

Tornados ripped through city streets, through lava, through crowds, sending people flying through the air only to be reintroduced to gravity and its consequences. Mass hysteria took hold as the population of earth was exterminated.

Portals from hell were opened by Satan's corporeal body. Demons rose from the depths, claiming the souls of earth's inhabitants.

The war is forever ongoing, but this round was over before it even started. He felt his body being moved for him. A single tear rolled down Mark's cheek.

THE STORM

Vivian Hampton, thirty-four-year-old single mother of two, pulled into the church parking lot. She had spent a lot of time speaking with God ever since she was diagnosed with breast cancer last year. She pulled the silver Volvo into the first available parking spot and slipped the shifter into park. Fumbling, she retrieved her purse and rummaged through the contents before finding the aluminum flask.

Okay. So, God wasn't the only thing she was turning to these days. But cancer was wrecking her life, not to mention her perfect tits.

"Jesus, please forgive me," she said, before taking a long slug of the Five O'clock Vodka inside. She grimaced, forcing the liquid down with a hard swallow. One more burning gulp later and she returned the shiny, metallic container back to her purse and pulled her keys from the ignition.

She stepped out of the car and forced on the best fake smile she could muster. *Here we go. Please, don't let me die. I don't want to die. I have already lost everything. Why are you doing this to me?* Vivian tried her hardest to clear her mind and walked to the church.

33

She opened the front door with a metallic click. The foyer floor was a beautiful white marble with golden cross inlays. The walls were coated in a multitude of colors, the majority a bright red. Vivian followed the stone pathway into the massive worship room. Beautiful stained-glass windows lined the walls, depicting various scenes from the Bible.

Light shone through the multi-colored windows, illuminating the church's extravagant interior. A life-size golden Jesus on a cross hung directly above the pulpit. Vivian approached the prie- dieu and again fumbled through her purse. This time she retrieved the new-looking Bible, and after setting her purse on the floor next to her, she knelt.

She placed the book on the rail in front of her and lowered her head to pray. She quietly mouthed the words even though Saint Augustine was currently empty.

"Dear Lord, please... Please, please let me live. I am on my knees for you. Please," she said.

Footsteps clacked on the hard floor; she looked toward the sound.

"Vivian, welcome back. It's good to see you," Father Marcus said. "I'm sorry I interrupted you."

"No, Father, no interruption at all. I'm glad you're here."

Vivian stood and greeted Father Marcus. Her arm snapped out clumsily to grab hold of his hand. A small pair of skeleton keys fell from his grasp.

"Oh, please, forgive me, Father," she said, grabbing his hand and kissing it.

"Please, my child, relax. Would you like to go to confession? There are two others waiting. I would be happy to hear you out."

"That would be wonderful, Father. Thank you."

Truthfully, she loathed confession. She hated everything about churches and the people that went to them. She would much rather be getting laid, but none of that would happen if she died. Come on Vivian... You can fake your way through this. Soon, you'll be back to normal.

They quietly left the worship room and proceeded to the confessional booth at the side of the room. Vivian sat on the bench outside, next to two other middle-aged women waiting for their turn to confess. They quietly greeted each other with nods and smiles. Vivian didn't recognize either of them, but she was relatively new to religion. Religion was a common side effect of cancer, and it was no different in her case.

Roughly thirty minutes passed before it was her turn. The previous woman exited the booth and departed. Vivian stood and entered the dark-brown wooden booth.

Hearing her enter, Father Marcus began the typical prayer. "Please begin," he said.

"Forgive me, Father, for I have sinned. It has been over twenty years since my last confession."

"That's quite a long time. I am sure you have much to confess."

"I do. You see, I have recently been diagnosed with breast cancer. I am very scared. I don't want to die. I want so many things from my life."

"Aye. Have you prayed on it a lot? Have you been a good Christian?" he asked.

"I have prayed every night of my life," she lied, rolling her eyes in disgust.

There was no reply from the Father. A wooden door clacked shut, somewhere close. Vivian jumped.

"Father Marcus?"

Again, no reply. The sound of keys jingling broke the silence. The lock on her side of the booth clicked as the key, now inside it, turned.

"Father? What's going on?"

Vivian grabbed the handle on the door and began to turn it. The door wouldn't budge.

"Father?" she said, panic stricken. "Father... What the fuck is going on?"

She heard the other door open and close again.

"Oh thank God. I'm stuck in here. Please get me out." Stricken with panic, Vivian pounded on the door.

She screamed, "Let me out! Get me the hell out of here!

Suddenly the lights flickered before dying completely. The confessional wall between her and where Father Marcus was supposed to be slid open. The booth was pitch black and suddenly very hot inside. Vivian stood and slammed her shoulder against the door. Her heart pounded rapidly, forcing her blood through her veins.

"Father Marcus, help!"

"There is no use screaming," a voice whispered right in her ear. "This is what you get for being a whore. *Voluptuous Vivian.* Isn't that what they called you after you got your new tits?"

"Fuck off! I don't know who the hell you are, but I am going to call the police! Father?"

"No. No, I don't think you are," the voice said as Vivian rattled the door.

Unable to open the door, Vivian searched through her purse in the dark. Her hands glanced over the contents. *There. There it is.* With the flick of her thumb, a spark jetted from the top of the lighter she had retrieved. The flame illuminated the blackened room like a can light at a rock concert. Unfortunately for Vivian, the light impaired her already night-adjusted vison. Fuck.

A long, slender finger slid out from behind the flame.

That wasn't a finger... That was a claw. A claw with a very long, very sharp nail.

"Oh, Jesus Christ!" she screamed.

"At least your tits won't kill you! Goodbye Vivian." As the voice spoke her name, the claw closed around the flame and extinguished it. The lighter ripped from her grasp. The thick, hot air began to fill her with panic. Her heart pounded.

Something clacked against the booth's wooden floor, moving closer to her.

"Oh Jesus."

Sharp claws struck her arms. Blood escaped the new wounds wetting her clothes. Pain rushed in and took the blood's place.

She screamed—

It was too late. The claws ripped through her skin, through the muscle in her neck. The creature grabbed hold of the spine buried deep in her neck. She felt the fingers grip it tightly. Vivian stood frozen, only able to blink as the life drained from her body.

The creature pulled, breaking her neck. The grip released at the sound of the snapping bones. Vivian's body slumped to the floor, her eyes filled with eternal darkness.

Vivian Hampton's home, Key Largo, Florida—Tuesday, August 18, 1992 Six days before...

Dex sat conversing with his sister, Mary, in the kitchen of their beach-front home.

"What the hell are we going to do, Dex?" Mary asked.

"Nothing. Mom has done this before. You know how she is. I'm sure she'll be home soon. I'm sure she is just out with the dickbag of the week," Dex replied.

"I get it... Mom's a whore. But still... she's never left us alone during hurricane season. Hurricane Andrew is only a few days out. We can't stay here. I don't want to fucking die, asshole!"

"Oh my God... Over-react much? I'm seventeen, Mary. If she isn't back in a couple days, we can just get in the Jeep and I'll drive us out of here. I have a few hundred bucks saved up so we can eat and stuff. Relax already. You're such a drama queen."

"Fine but..." Mary said anxiously.

An emergency alert warning broke over the television. "Yeah, yeah. I get it. It's windy. Stop playing that annoying
sound," Dex said.

Mary slammed an elbow into his ribs. "Shut up. This is serious."

A computerized voice spoke as the words scrolled across the screen. The two, now silent, leaned closer to the TV

"The U.S. Weather Service has issued a severe storm warning for areas in the southern panhandle of Florida. Expect winds of up to forty miles per hour tonight growing to fifty tomorrow," the voice said.

"The U.S. Weather Service is issuing an evacuation for the following counties: Miami-Dade, Broward, Palm Beach, Martin, St. Lucie, Indian River..."

"Dex, I really think we should go. They're evacuating the whole coast," Mary said.

"I know but I'm not leaving Mom here and spending all my money for no reason. It isn't even that bad out. Look."

He stood and walked to the sliding glass door. The sky was a bright blue and peppered with clouds. They were moving relatively fast, but all of the trees were still upright. So how bad could it really be?

"It's not even bad. The waves are still below the seawall. We are good for another couple days. Trust me."

"Fine, but you are getting us pizza for dinner tonight! And I want mushrooms!"

Dex laughed and messed up her hair with his hand. "Stop... Stop!"

Vivian Hampton's home, Key Largo, Florida—Friday, August 21, 1992—5:00am
Three days before...

Waves crashed violently over the concrete seawall. Set after set bashed against the concrete, sending hundreds of gallons of saltwater flying into the air. The wind had been howling since late Tuesday night, but not like this.

Dex awoke to the sounds of rattling siding and the whir of wind whistling through the cracks in the closed windows. He was

nervous about getting trapped in the storm but had been through worse. The last hurricane had been just like this and then drifted away into nothingness. He hoped that hurricane Andrew would do the same, even though the likelihood of that was small.

Dex rolled over in his bed and reached for the remote on his nightstand but discovered the whole stand was empty as he swept his arm across its surface. A fresh blast of sea air ripped in through his window, flying across the stand.

Jesus, that's some strong wind. It knocked all my shit onto the floor.

He reached down and poked around in the darkness, like a blind man, before he found it. Gripping its rubber keys and plastic body, he flipped himself back into bed. He fumbled for a moment before finding and finally pressing the power button.

The television clicked on. MTV raged to life. Ugly Kid Joe's *Everything About You* blared. He'd obviously forgotten to turn the TV down before he crashed. His thumb jammed on the volume button and began flipping through the channels, searching for news.

He found the local ABC news channel. Peter Jennings was intensely reporting on the approaching hurricane.

"Overnight the wind speeds have seemingly increased exponentially. Andrew wasn't expected to make landfall until August twenty eighth. In an unprecedented manner, Andrew has now morphed into a Category Five storm. The latest analysis now puts Andrew crashing onto the shore near Homestead, Florida, sometime on the morning of the twenty fourth. If you haven't already begun your evacuation, I urge you to do so now," Jennings said.

Water splashed against the window of Dex's room.

Maybe this was more serious than he thought. *Where the hell is Mom?*

An emergency alert came over the TV, interrupting his train of thought. It reiterated much of the same information Peter Jennings had already gone over, but then a familiar face filled the screen.

Father Marcus?

"Citizens of Key Largo," he said, "I have prayed for all of you. You are my flock, my friends. I care a great deal for you and wish to open my house to you. For those of you who have not yet

evacuated, I fear that moment for escape has passed. There is no Ark from Noah to save us from the Devil's fury that is surely inbound.

"Please, wait no longer. Come join me in the storm shelter beneath Saint Augustine's. There is plenty of food and water for all those left in Key Largo. Wait no longer. The storm is coming."

The feeling of impending doom scared the shit out of Dex. Alone, in his room, he sat staring at Father Marcus' face. His crooked smile was untrustworthy, like that of a used car salesman. But at least the church was an option. He rose from his bed to peer out the covered window.

Before reaching the window, the glass exploded. Shards of the sharp glass flew through the air. Some of the pieces struck Dex in the face, ripping gashes both large and small, and Dex screamed. Blood trickled from the wounds. More glass shards pounded his body.

Something crashed repeatedly into the house. *Thud. Thud. Thud.*

What the fuck?

Dex wiped the blood from his face, and a flash of red smashed into the broken window, stopped only by the thick wood frame of the small window.

He flinched. "Holy shit!"

Pinned to the window was a STOP sign. Its reflective white letters lit up from the light of the television.

"Fuck—I think we waited too long."

"Mary! Mary! Get up!" Dex yelled.

"What the hell, Dex? Leave me alo... Holy shit! What happened to your face?"

"The storm busted out the window and I got all cut up. Listen, there is no time to argue. Get up and pack a bag right now. You have to HURRY!"

"Oh my God! Alright. I'll hurry. Are you going to be okay?"

"I'll be fine. The cuts aren't too deep I don't think. I'll go clean up in the other bathroom," Dex said.

"Where are we going?"

"There isn't time to talk about this right now. Please Mary, go!" he screamed over the howling wind.

Dex saw the worry on Mary's face. What thirteen-year-old wouldn't be? After all, they were trapped in the path of an impending hurricane and their mom had been gone, presumably fucking some random dude, for almost a week.

Dex waited until Mary left the room to go clean himself up. He slowly pulled a few pieces of embedded glass out of his face and chest. His face contorted in pain as he tugged on each piece. Blood trickled down his face. He grabbed a white hand towel and soaked it in hot water. After he removed each piece, he pressed it to the area to help stop the bleeding.

More often than not, the pressure from the towel revealed another piece of glass hidden under the skin's surface.

"Ouch. Damn it!" he yelled as the towel revealed yet another shard. This one required a pair of tweezers to remove. Carefully, he plucked out the shrapnel. More blood leaked from his face. He thought that was the last one, though, and at least that provided a small bit of relief.

He wrung out the blood-soaked towel, re-wet it with fresh water, and gave his face one last rub, just to make sure he got everything. Just as he finished, the lights went out.

Fuck.

"Mary! Hurry up. The power is out. We need to get out of here now!" he yelled up the stairs.

Another sound of breaking glass came from upstairs. "Mary?" he yelled up the stairs. Footsteps pounded down the stairs and she flew into view. "You ready?" he asked, relieved that she was okay.

"Yeah, that was the window in my room. Are we going to be okay?"

"We'll be fine. You just have to do what I say. Can you do that? Can you be brave?"

Mary nodded, her bag clasped tightly in her right hand, a teddy bear clutched tightly in the other.

"Good girl. Let's go," he said.

They rushed through the house, making their way to the garage, and Mary followed closely behind Dex. Things slammed into the exterior of the house. Dex hoped they could get to the church okay.

Seconds later, the two leapt into the front seats of Dex's Jeep. It was nowhere as nice as his mom's, but it was his and he liked it. He reached up and clicked the button on the garage door opener. Nothing happened. He clicked it harder, a few more times.

Nothing...

"Shit. The power is out. Hold on, Mary, I have to get out and open the door."

Mary clung to the stuffed bear in her lap, squeezing it so tight that it looked like it might pop at any moment. Dex patted her head and hopped out. He rushed to the door and ripped it open, revealing the fresh load of Hell outside.

Water flew sideways through the air, bringing with it debris of all shapes and sizes. A palm frond whipped in front of his face. He leaned out of the garage, tracking the larger pieces and was promptly struck by another. He returned to the Jeep and looked at Mary.

"Hold on, kiddo. This is going to be a rough ride." "Where are we going?" she asked again.

"Oh, sorry. Father Marcus was on TV and said Saint Augustine's had plenty of room in the shelter and loads of food and water. I think it's too dangerous to leave the Keys, so..."

"Oh, good. That's not too far, either."

"That's a good thing too."

Dex turned the Jeep over and it roared to life. With one more rev, he slammed the stick shift into first and dumped the clutch. The Jeep lurched from the garage as the tires broke and regained traction.

Once out of the safety of the garage, the Jeep bounced over the piles of debris that covered the ground. Dex gripped the wheel, white-knuckle tight. He swerved rather expertly around the larger objects while busting through the others.

As the vehicle changed direction, so did the rain. The open-topped vehicle quickly soaked with a mix of rain and the salty seawater. Mary was now pleading to hurry. Dex could see that she was soaked, as was he, but she was shivering already.

He shifted and slammed his foot back onto the pedal, bottoming it out on the floorboards. The engine revved. Dex reached to turn up the open-top vehicle's heater just as a telephone pole cracked under the pressure of the wind. The pole toppled and slammed to the ground directly in the Jeep's path.

"Shit!" Dex screamed, jerking the wheel hard to the left and slamming on the brakes. "Hold on!"

The Jeep slid, hydroplaning across the water's surface. It spun out of control and slammed violently into a yellow curb lining the road's edge. The rear passenger's side dropped down, stopping the Jeep. The vehicle rested awkwardly, the nose perched much higher than the rear.

Dex checked to make sure Mary was okay. She was, so he unfastened her seatbelt and they jumped out. He grabbed their bags. And they ran. Just a few blocks from Saint Augustine's, they ran hard. Occasionally they tripped and stumbled, but neither fell.

Before they knew it, they were standing in the parking lot of the church. They pushed on, scanning the lot for flying debris, ducking what flew near them. Then he saw it.

"Oh my God. Look, Mary. Mom's Jeep."

"Awesome, let's get in there and find out why the hell she left us at home ALONE!"

"Relax. First let's get safe, then we'll deal with the other stuff."

"Fine," she said, picking up the pace.

They burst through the church doors with a percussive bang.

Dex and Mary were welcomed into Saint Augustine's with open arms by Father Marcus. They were issued a cot as well as a few towels and some snacks to tide them over until dinner. The shelter was not much more than a large concrete bunker underneath the church. It served its purpose, though. It felt... safe.

Dex and Mary set up their cots together. There must have been a couple hundred other townsfolk there already. Many were settled in and sat conversing with each other, talking about all manner of things.

Prior to setting up their cots, both Mary and he had searched the area for their mother. Neither found any sign of her. They decided that she had to be here somewhere and they would take turns searching for her after they dried off and settled in.

Shortly after they were dry-ish, Father Marcus paid them a visit.

"Welcome, my children," he opened with. "I trust you are settling in okay?"

"Yes, Father," Dex said. Without hesitation he blurted, "Have you seen my mother? Her Jeep is outside, but I can't find her."

"I did see her, several days ago. Around the fourteenth, I believe. She was here for prayers and confession. I waited for her to finish praying, but she never showed up for confession. I assumed that she left afterwards. Ask around, though. This shelter is large and I don't get around well. It is possible that I missed her."

Father Marcus retrieved something from his pocket. He opened his hand and presented his open palm to them. Two butterscotch candies and a pair of skeleton keys lay in his palm.

"Please, have a piece of candy," Father Marcus said.

The children obliged and took the candies, leaving the keys. "Thank you, Father," they said.

They hurriedly unwrapped the sweets and popped them into their mouths. Over the next couple days, Mary and he took turns walking around the shelter, looking for their mother. Unfortunately, no one they spoke with had any recollection of seeing her. At least they were warm, dry, and safe.

Until the generator stopped. The lights flickered, and... died.

Saint Augustine Church, Key Largo, Florida—Sunday, August 23, 1992
One day before...

Father Marcus spoke, "Fear not, my parishioners, candles are being distributed as I speak."

Sure enough, candles began to light tiny patches of the shelter one or two at a time. This didn't stop children from screaming and crying. No, it incited the raucous noise. Sounds echoed deafeningly off the cold stone walls.

A scream resonated off the high ceiling. This one wasn't from a child, but rather, from a man. It was immediately followed by a loud *snap*.

"What the hell was that?" Dex asked.

"I don't know. I think it came from somewhere above. Maybe up in the ceiling supports," Mary said.

Sounds of wood creaking filled the air. And a gust of wind ripped through the basement shelter, blowing out all of the freshly lit candles. Several more *snaps* came from above, frightening the parishioners. Dex heard them gasping.

"What the fuck?" Dex said. "Let's move to the walls in case the ceiling collapses."

He stood and felt Mary do the same. The air was again still inside the room. Something dripped down Dex's left, arm and he instinctively reached out to wipe it off.

A viscous liquid with a new, strange odor filled his nostrils.

What the fuck...

The candles in the room lit, one at a time. He fumbled with the packet of matches they'd been given and struck a match and put it to the wick. A small area around them illuminated. Mary gasped.

"Look at your arm, Dex. Is that blood?"

"What? No. Don't be stu..." his voice trailed off. The liquid that dripped down his arm was a deep red. Not like a nose bleed. He'd had his fair share of those. This red was different. Darker. Thicker.

Another volley of drops struck his arm. Shocked, he jerked it away from the drips. He raised his candle up and looked into the darkness. He couldn't see a damn thing.

"Shit. Can you tell where it's coming from?" he asked. "No. I can't see a fucking thing," she answered. "Mary... Watch your mouth. The Father is in here somewhere," he reprimanded.

"Sorry."

"I have an idea. Stand up on your cot. I'll give you my candle and raise you up on my shoulders. I don't want whatever this shit is dripping on me all night."

"Okay, I'm ready," she said.

Dex hoisted her up and she raised the candles high and waved them around searching for the source. They lit up very little.

"What do you see, Mary?"

"Nothing. It's way too dark. Oh fuck! Dex! Help me! Put me down now!" she screamed.

Dex dropped her. She was still screaming and shaking violently.

"What is it? What did you see?" Mary wrapped herself tightly around Dex's torso, bawling. "Mary, tell me what you saw."

"There is a man—hanging—up there," she sputtered. "What?" he asked. "A dead guy, Dex. Some dude hung himself and is swinging up there," she cried.

"Then this is *blood*? Oh, Jesus!" Dex screamed. "Father Marcus!"

More and more candles were lit, illuminating the room better. Dex hugged his sister tightly. Both of them tucked their heads into each other, blocking out the horrific sight of the dangling man.

Screaming echoed off the walls as the brightness increased. Dex pulled Mary closer but raised his head to look at what had caused the commotion.

"Oh God! Don't look, Mary."

Three groups of men hung some fifteen or so feet above the crowd's head. Dex felt sick. The men swung back and forth, occasionally bumping into one another. Dex counted six. Six men in each group. Six in each. Six, six, and six.

Parents all across the room covered their children's eye. These were not just random men dangling from the ceiling. Dex recognized them as fathers, brothers, and sons to some of the others.

Chaos erupted. Those with sense charged the steps that had brought them down into the shelter. Two or three wide, they ascended the stone steps. Panic filled their candlelit faces.

The room was deafeningly loud and filled with the sense of impending doom. Dex watched the first few reach the top of the stairs. They fumbled with the knob, but it didn't open. They slammed their shoulders into the door. The door stayed sealed shut.

Several new men took the others' places, beating on the locked door. They slammed and kicked at it. Some hit it so hard they broke bones. Those injured were carried down the stairs, back through the crowd below. Back to where their families were, where their cots sat. Back to where the bodies hung.

Dex and Mary watched as the men's injuries were treated as best they could be with no medical supplies. What kind of shelter has no medical supplies?

A new voice shouted over the roaring crowd. "Stop, please. Stop! Stop!" the man's voice screamed.

Somehow, it gained the attention of the entire room, even over the banging and panicking.

"This isn't working. The door is stuck. Likely from something above. Probably the storm. We can't just sit here and let the kids see these men hanging from the ceiling. Let's cut them down and get them out of sight."

"Has anyone seen Father Marcus? He may know if there is a ladder down here," the man said.

No one answered him.

A woman from the crowd brought the man a long fiberglass pole.

"This was in the back. I think they hang Christmas lights with it," she said.

"Thank you," the man replied. "This helps, actually."

Dex watched him pull a large pocket knife out and unfold it. The man cut a strip of sheet off of the cot next to him and used it to secure the knife to the pole.

"Grab a few blankets and the strongest of you will have to get under the men one at a time and catch the bodies as I cut them loose. They are already dead," the man said. "So it won't hurt them if you miss. Just don't get caught under them."

Horror filled Dex's eyes and the men took their places. The man raised the pole toward the first rope. He touched the knife to the rope and pushed the pole forward.

"ENOUGH!" a voice said echoing through the room. The church bells began to clang, signaling midnight. The sound was deafening. The candles flickered. Another gust ripped through the room and extinguished the flames—*again*.

Saint Augustine Church, Key Largo, Florida—Monday, August 24, 1992
The day of...

A glow of fire illuminated the area around the top of the stairs. A man clad in a dark robe entered the room and walked down several steps and stopped. A large orange flame engulfed his right hand. It danced back and forth, casting horrifying shadows over the room.

Shit... Dex eyed the staff in his left hand. It was a long golden rod with three bars crossing it at the top. Each bar was slightly shorter than the one below it. The staff itself was nearly as tall as the robed man that possessed it.

"Let us begin," the robed man said.

The man raised the staff high into the air and clacked it onto the stone steps. A dark wave of energy shot out across the room. The bags of flesh hanging from the ceiling exploded into a fine, red mist that rained down onto the crowd below them.

Dex and Mary screamed, as did the rest of the crowd. The red liquid rained over everyone and covered them from head to toe in blood.

"SILENCE!" the robed man commanded. "Kneel before me."

Some of the crowd did just that as looks of terror covered their faces. Others froze in place.

Dex was one of the latter, Mary the former.

"KNEEL!" the man commanded again, striking the stone with the heel of the staff.

That was all it took. Another wave of the same dark energy ripped through the crowd, much lower this time. It tore their legs out from under them, causing them to fall onto the blood-drenched floor. A second wave of energy crashed into Dex's body and was quickly absorbed.

Where the man once stood, Dex watched as the robe fell to the floor, empty. The fire dropped to the floor as well but still burned brightly.

Dex stood. He saw Mary look up at him with a what-the-fuck look.

"What are you doing?" she asked him.

Dex simply raised a single finger and pressed it across his lips. "Shhh."

Dex walked to the front of the shelter and ascended the stairs to where the staff stood glimmering next to the flames. He knelt and retrieved the two skeleton keys from the pocket of the robe. Dex clutched the staff and looked over the crowd of kneeling, shuddering heathens.

He took the keys and separated them from the ring.

"These keys were once *my* keys. My keys that opened the gates of Heaven. Now they are the keys to *your* Hell!"

One at a time he slid them into the two keyholes in the staff and gave each a quarter turn, locking them into place. Dex raised the staff high into the air and continued to speak.

"I was there for the massacre of Matthew. I was there for the obliteration of Sodom and Gomorrah. I was there for the torment of Job. I was there for the massacre of the Innocents. I was there for the ten plagues of Egypt. I was there for the flood of Noah. I was there for God's judgment against Jerusalem. I was there for the crucifixion of Christ. And I will be there for the Lake of Fire, when Hell comes to Earth. I will be there long after you have perished.

"FOR I AM ABADDON. I am destruction. I am Lord of the Pit. King of Locusts. I am the Destroyer!"

Fire rose and covered Dex. It swirled around him, engulfing him in his entirety. His human flesh melted away leaving only Abaddon.

The fire died down around Abaddon's hooved feet. His scepter now blackened, glowed a fiery orange in places. He stood some nine or so feet tall now. A set of giant bat-like wings sprang out from his back. Claws replaced fingers. Red, veiny skin replaced pale flesh. The only thing that remained from where Dex's body once stood was charred stone.

Abaddon leapt from the great stone stairs. His wings flapped, cushioning his landing. Abaddon kicked those close enough to kick. Their puny human carcasses crushed like balsa wood. He raised his fiery scepter above his head and swung it. It crashed into five, six, seven at a time, their bodies breaking and instantly set ablaze.

"Your kind will never survive. You are far too trusting. Look at me when I kill you. You trusted me when I looked like your beloved Father Marcus." Abaddon smashed a wriggling carcass next to him with his great hoof.

"Mary. My dear fool, Mary." Abaddon clomped over to her. "You trusted me too. Just as your filthy whore of a mother did. You believed that your frail shit of a brother, weak little Dex, would save you.

"Let me say this... Much like your mother, and all the humans that have had the displeasure of crossing my path, you were wrong."

Abaddon raised his great staff above Mary and paused briefly, "Goodbye, Mary. Say hello to your mother for me!"

The staff swung down, chased by a flaming comet. It smashed into Mary, making her head explode. A fine, red mist sprayed across the already grim room. Abaddon swung time and time again, his staff colliding with those in its path. The carnage was nothing short of complete destruction.

Abaddon wrecked on until the entire shelter was completely ablaze, while outside, hurricane Andrew did the same, smashing and crushing all of southern Florida.

What was left, Key Largo, Florida—Wednesday, August 26, 1992 Two days after...

From above, rescue workers dug into the pile of rubble that was once Saint Augustine's Church. Rescue dogs barked at the smell of a human body trapped below. A male voice called for the workers.

"Help me. I'm trapped down here," the voice shouted. "We are coming, son, hold on," the fireman shouted back. They broke through to the entrance of the shelter several

minutes later. There, on the steps, lay the body of the trapped teen.

He coughed as the debris rained down on his battered body. The fireman reached in and pulled the boy out.

"What's your name, son?" he asked.

"Dex," he replied.

Dex sat up after they pulled him out. He clung to a broken scepter in one hand and a pair of skeleton keys in the other. He scanned his surroundings and found only four firemen and a search-and-rescue dog for as far as he could see.

He stood, gripping the scepter tightly and plunged its jagged end into the neck of the closest fireman. Blood sprayed from the man's neck as he collapsed to the wet ground. Fast as lightning, Dex did the same to the other three firemen. They were all dead in less than a minute.

Dex looked at the dog. They locked eyes for a moment. The dog whimpered and sat, submitting to him. Dex walked over and knelt next to it. He ran his bloody fingers through the German shepherd's soft fur. The dog began to pant happily.

Dex grabbed its head and twisted with all his might. The dog's head separated from its body. Blood sprayed through the air and the dog's body collapsed.

What was left, Key Largo, Florida—Wednesday, August 26, 1992

A news helicopter flew over what was left of Key Largo. The pilot communicated with the cameraman in the back via headset. Both scoured the wreckage.

"Hey, Carl. Look over there. What is that?" the pilot asked. "Looks like a dog. Maybe a German shepherd," Carl said. "Shall we set down and save it?" the pilot asked.

"Hell yeah. That would make great news."

The pilot began to lower the chopper. The shepherd stopped and sat, looking up at the helicopter as it landed.

"Go get him, Carl. I'll film."

The pilot grabbed the camera, switched it on and placed it atop his shoulder. His eye pressed tightly to the viewfinder; he zoomed in on the pup. Steadying himself, the camera lens whirred, focusing.

The coarse fur whipped to and fro, like tall grass in a summer breeze. The dog locked eyes with the pilot through the camera lens. It crouched, eyes changing from blue to blood red. A smile spread across its face.

"Carl, stop!"

THE PERFECT PRESENT

I t was a frigid morning in Detroit. Jesus Christ... Seven months a fucking year, it was a frigid morning in Detroit. Darren Childs woke up. The snow outside reflected and intensified the winter sun. This was not where he thought he would be at thirty- eight years old. Living in his bitch-of-a-mother's spare room.

Another day for a pathetic, worthless shit... He wiped the sleep from his eyes and yawned. His foul morning breath filled his nostrils as he exhaled. Darren stretched his arm out, searching for his glasses on his heavily worn side table.

He knocked several McDonald's cups over. The foul stagnant fluid spilled onto the nightstand.

"Fuck!" he yelled as he slammed his fist onto the table. More plastic drink cups jumped into the air. The sticky fluid splashed on his bed. Darren flicked the liquid off his hand and dried it on his bed sheet.

He stood and stretched before picking up a piss-stained pair of underwear off the pile of trash at the foot of his bed. He pulled them on and walked out of his room. His feet crunched across an open bag of Cheetos in the hallway. Darren lifted a leg and blasted a foul cloud of gas.

"Ha!" he laughed aloud.

Darren descended the stairs toward the sound of pans banging in the kitchen. He rounded the corner, scratching his chest. His mother, Cyndi, was bent down reaching for a rusted frying pan in the lower cupboard.

She was dressed in her whore outfit again. Cheap, overly tight, torn-crotch, blue jeans. She wore an open-top, low-cut shirt and, of course—like a true whore—no bra. It might have been fine if she was twenty, but she wasn't. She was fifty-six years old.

"Jesus Christ, Ma... Put a fuckin' bra on. Your tits are hangin' like oranges in tube socks. You ain't turnin' nobody on with them things!" he ridiculed.

She turned her head and looked back at him, a look of disgust emblazoned on her face.

"Look who's talkin'. Looks like you rubbed a stick-a-butter on them undies," she fired back. "Ain't you gotta work?"

He did have to work. But it wasn't his normal job. It was Christmas Eve. He had his *other* job.

"Yeah. Not 'til late though," he confirmed.

"Good. So you have time?" she asked.

Without waiting for a reply, she moved toward Darren. She kneeled in front of him and gently tugged his underwear down. She took him into her mouth—

Why...? I don't like this... I don't like this... I don't like this... Fuck! Why am I getting hard? This is so fucked! I never should have let this happen. I was so young though. Is this MY fault? I know she has been lonely since Dad left her, but come on.

Sucking and fucking and doing this shit with your son is so—fucked! Why did he have to leave? He was an asshole, but at least he never did this! Why is this exciting me? I shouldn't be so turned on.

Fuck. Why am I letting this feel good? Why did it feel so good when I was fourteen? Why did she have to ruin Christmas? A blowjob is not a gift for your son... If I could have just told her no then... Maybe she wouldn't have kept doing this. Maybe... Oh...

Maybe if I hadn't let her do THIS, then I wouldn't have a fucking kid with my mother! Oh... Oh... Fuck...

"I'm g-gonna—" he stuttered and took hold of her hair. He pulled her in tightly.

What is wrong with me?

Cyndi pulled up his underwear and stood. She returned to her duties as though nothing disturbing had taken place at all. Disgusted, Darren walked out of the kitchen and hurried to his room. Tears rolled down his face and dripped across his crooked smile.

Looks like it's gonna be another screwed-up Christmas.

Walking back to his room, he picked up the bag of Cheetos. Grabbing a fistful, he opened his mouth and tossed them in. A cockroach crawled out from inside the bag onto his wrist. Darren flicked it away and continued eating.

He dressed, no shower, and returned to the downstairs.

"I'll be back later," he said to his mother before closing the door.

There, in the driveway, sat his 1970-something Ford Econoline van. It was a putrid, light pea-green color. Well, the parts that weren't rusted were anyway. He kicked through the December snow and shuffled his way to the driver's door.

It opened with a loud creaking noise. Darren entered and started the engine. *Time to go see what the day brings.* He fastened his seatbelt, put the van in drive, and pressed down on the accelerator.

The van lurched into the street and he drove off toward the local Walmart. Walmart had been a favorite place of his to go "looking" for his special projects. *The beautiful thing about Walmart is the goddamn place never closes. So where else would I go to look for some shit-ass parent that waits until the last minute to go out and buy presents?*

Yeah, yeah. I know. They are doing their best to provide for their children. Maybe they can't afford to buy presents or food or whatever. I'm not Barack mother-fuckin' Obama. And I sure ain't that saggy-titted bitch Hillary Clinton. A parent's got a responsibility to take care of their child. They have to put them first. Not sometimes. Not once in a while. All the fucking time! I am so sick of shitty parents taking advantage of their kids.

"No, Jimmy, you can't have that Transformer. No, Bobby, you can't have that Butterfinger. Come on, Darren, just relax. It will feel good, just relax for Mommy."

No! Never again! Not this year. I'm gonna find her and I will teach that bitch a lesson!

Darren mashed the gas pedal to the floor. The van coughed out a cloud of black smoke and sped faster down the street. In no time he found himself arriving at Walmart. As he pulled in, he looked

for a parking space that would be sufficient, one that had a good view of people arriving and one that would allow him to not stick out like a sore thumb in his rust bucket of a van.

That was not going to be easy. The parking lot was packed with herds of cars. Nearly every make and model was represented in the lot.

Darren circled the rows like cowboys wrangling cattle. He inspected each vehicle and looked for signs that the owner was— *Holy Shit!*

There it was, just sitting there! A piece-of-shit fuckin' beater van. It's fucked-up paint fit right in at the parking lot in Walmart. The afternoon sun was setting, so Darren drove the van around to the front. The van sat parked in a clearly marked handicapped spot. No handicap plates, no handicap placard.

Even from his own vehicle, he could see that there, in the third-row seat, was an unfastened child seat. Just sitting there. He backed his van into a parking space that bordered the lot's edge and turned off the engine. Darren reached under the seat and retrieved a small, black CaseLogic cassette case from under the seat. He fumbled with the zipper.

Once open, he selected a cassette labeled "Christmas" and slid it into the in-dash cassette player. Bing Crosby's voice broke the silence as he sang, *"It's Beginning to Look a Lot Like Christmas."* Darren leaned back in the van's bucket seat and began to bob his head along with the music. He faded into thought, remembering the first time—

"She had been such a foul cunt, the way she glared at her kid. She was supposed to love her child. Like a mother should. Instead, she looked at her with disdain. She walked out of Walmart, practically dragging her youngest by the arm. The small girl couldn't have been more than seven.

The news announced later that her name was Suzy Stephens and her mom's was Hollie Winters. The fucking bitch couldn't even keep her legs closed long enough to land a husband. Hollie jerked little Suzy's arm a few more times, dragging her to the car. She puffed on a slim cigarette and blew the smoke right at Suzy.

What a bitch. She pissed me off so much... I got out of the vehicle when I couldn't take it anymore. I wanted her dead right there, and I didn't give a shit who saw. I stormed right at them as they walked to the car. I reached into the back of my pants, grabbing hold of the K- Bar knife that I had tucked in there earlier. I was on them in no time.

I went to draw the knife. This was it. I was going to help this poor child. I made one last step toward Hollie. She didn't even see me. I could have stabbed her ten times before she knew what hit her. That is, if it wasn't for the ice.

During that last step, I slipped on a sheet of slick, black ice. My shoulder collided with Hollie's. I shoved the knife back into the sheath just before I smacked the asphalt, hard! I was embarrassed, but what pissed me off more was what that bitch said.

"Watch where the fuck you are going, dipshit," she balked. "Dumbass."

Right there, I knew: this bitch had to die! I watched from my back as she jerked Suzy's arm and drug her to her van. I had been too distracted by rage to notice that Hollie was dressed very nicely, and poor Suzy was wearing clothes that were much too small for her. She looked so cold. Hollie really didn't give a shit about her.

This year *had* to be Suzy's best Christmas. It HAD to be!

I picked myself up off the ground and carefully walked back to my van. Hollie drove past me and added insult to the ordeal by flipping me off. I was gonna make that whore eat those fingers. I brushed the snow and gravel off my backside and got in the van.

I turned the key, it roared to life, and I slammed it into gear. I couldn't risk losing her. I tailed her from a distance, so she wouldn't see me. I felt like MacGyver or some shit. My heart pounded in my chest. It was exhilarating. I trailed her for a few miles until she made a left turn into Rosebloom Trailer Park. What a dump.

I could see that the complex was very small. Bags of trash were scattered across "lawns" like ornaments. I didn't want her to see me, so I parked at an apartment complex across the street and watched to make sure she didn't leave. I waited until the sun went down. Then, it was time.

I had worn the brown Carhartt overalls and matching jacket I bought with the money I stole from Ma's purse. Snow had started to fall again. This was exactly the white Christmas I had hoped for. It took ten or so minutes to find the vehicle that Hollie had drove off in. It was parked in front of a dilapidated trailer.

Blackish-gray shutters hung loosely from the un-curtained front window. They occasionally slapped against the trailer's aluminum siding. As I peered through the window, I could see clearly that the noise didn't even draw attention. I was sure that would work in my favor.

I took refuge in a row of bushes and spent some time watching the goings-on inside. Hollie could be seen shuffling through the house wearing only her bra and panties. What a slut. She walked to the refrigerator and removed a box of Franzia wine.

She poured herself a plastic NASCAR cup full of it. The box was obviously reaching empty, as Hollie tipped it, draining all of the remaining contents into the Jeff Gordon cup. She took a long drink from the glass and retrieved a candle from the drawer next to her. As she lit the candle, she twisted the holder. Two wings of four candles came into view. A menorah? She was using a menorah for candlelight? Jesus Christ...

I felt sick watching that bitch. She reached over to the shelf next to her and picked up a book. I strained to look at it. It was obviously one of them dirty chick books. *Golden Surrender*. It had that Fabio guy on the cover right under the name Heather Graham. That guy really needed a shirt! Nipple man! Ha! Yeah, I was a bit terrified that I knew who Fabio was but, fuck off. I was more surprised that she could fuckin' read than of what happened next.

She leaned back in her chair and unsnapped her bra. Uh... What the fuck was going on? The bra slid loosely down her arms as her breasts popped into sight. The worst thing came next, though. That filthy slut took a Jew candle from the middle of the menorah and shoved it right inside her pussy. The damn windows were open! Anyone could have seen!

That was it. It was my time to move. I sprang to my feet and ran across the street until I reached the bottom of the steps. I removed a paint scraper from my back pocket and quickly shoved it into the door jam. With one stiff smack of my hand on its butt, I was in.

I moved rapidly across the room. Funniest thing I ever saw. When I got to her, I punched her in the face as hard as I could, but she was still fuckin' herself with that Jew candle. HA! It popped out of her crotch like a cork from a pop gun. I almost pissed myself.

Anyways, she slumped right away and I put her in a headlock and drug that bitch out of the trailer. Little Suzy never even knew I was there. I got her outside. That was the hard part, until I realized that I'd parked the van across the street and forgot to move it here. Damnit!

What do I do? What do I do? I freaked the fuck out. I had this naked bitch in a choke hold, standing in the dark outside. There was a small snow bank next to her steps, so I punched her a few more times to make sure she was out. If she woke up, I could still bail, I supposed. And I ran for the van.

My heart raced as I jumped in the driver's seat. I turned the key and the engine came to life. I hoped that she didn't do the same! I drove as inconspicuously as possible to the trailer. When I got close, I saw she was still in the snow. Part of me wanted her to be gone 'cuz that would be a great news story. "Someone broke in my house—while I was fuckin' myself—with a big 'ol Jew candle —" Ha! That would have been so awesome.

Oh well. I jumped out of the van and slugged her in the face for good measure and drug her into the back of the van. Shit, I was scared, but it was exhilarating! I "quietly" slammed the back doors and hopped in the front. I didn't even remember to tie her up! I was such a dumb-ass. Luckily for me she didn't wake up.

I drove to Uncle Sam's storage. Uncle Sam was a used-up, fat, fuckin' Vet that couldn't let go of the four years he served. I'm sure he repaired staplers or some shit while he was in. He was curious why I rented such a big storage. I got one just big enough to get the van in, but I told him it was for a boat. I had to listen to his dumb-ass talk about all the fishin' he and his Army buds used to do. Whatever, piss off already.

When I got there, I hopped out and opened the door and drove the van inside. I closed the door and locked it from the inside. *Holy shit, I actually did it!* Now it was time for the good stuff. I grabbed the chest I had previously stored and drug it to the rear of the van. I retrieved the rope from inside it and opened the van doors. I had stashed a few construction lights, the kind that are on stands too. I plugged them in and aimed them in the back of the van.

I selected a few tools from the toy chest and hopped in the van with them. I quickly used the rope and tied up the *parent of the year*. I started to relax finally. I slapped her a few times to wake her up. It didn't work. I grabbed the ammonia inhalants I bought on Amazon and cracked one open. I didn't know how to use it so I shoved it right up her nose.

It worked!

That bitch screamed! Loud! I wrapped some rope around her mouth as a makeshift gag. I started to calm her down. I realized that she still had the ammonia in her nose. I bet that shit burned. I left it in —fuck it!

I grabbed my Mountain Dew from the cupholder up front and sat down next to her. We talked. Well, I talked. She freaked the fuck out! I told her all about how great of a mom she was. Oh, I forgot to mention that I was also cutting off her toes one at a time with a pair of rusty, old tin snips while I recited the merits of her parenting.

Blood spurted across the back of the van. After I snipped each, carefully painted I might add, toe off, I looked her right in the eyes while I poured rubbing alcohol onto each wound. Ha! Wouldn't want her to get an infection. Her face turned pale, from the shock I guessed. The ammonia seemed to keep her awake pretty good though.

"So, I couldn't help but notice back there in your trailer... You were fuckin' yourself. You know that your daughter is in that house right? Do you get off on knowing that she is that close to you while you are doing that? Well, since you like to shove shit in your cunt..." I unzipped my pants.

I wasn't gonna fuck her. She was a filthy bitch, but it sure freaked her out. Her eyes got all big and shit. That was when I knew I had all the power, and it felt good to use it. I was getting a little freaked out though. Beginner's nerves I guess. So I set aside shoving shit in her and moved to her fingers.

"Remember when you flipped me off bitch? Do it again." She shook her head no, obviously terrified, so I pulled out my K-bar and touched it to her left titty, right at the nipple. I yelled at the top of my lungs for her to flip me off. All she did was cry and shake her head no. So I made good on my threat. I sliced off her nipple like a piece of pepperoni. Ha! She screamed loud again. Well, as loud as one could scream with a mouth full of rope, no toes, and a missing nipple.

This time when I told her to flip me off—surprise, she did, I hacked off the other nipple. Why not? I was in charge. I laid the pair of nips on the wheel well behind me. I wasn't sure what I was gonna do with them, but I had time to figure it out.

Now, back to the fingers. I grabbed her right middle finger, the one she flipped me off with. I toyed with it for a minute. I bent it forward and backward through its range of motion until she relaxed just enough. Then I grabbed it as hard as I could and bent it backwards until it snapped at the base. Have you ever heard a finger bone crack? It's loud!

I moved her hand right in front of her face and wiggled the shit out of that busted finger. Man, that bitch sure did cry. Ha! Over the course of ten minutes or so I snapped each finger's bone, and then one at a time I cut through the flesh with my K-bar. Each finger plopped to the floor of the van, still wrigglin'! It was pretty funny.

I had an idea for them fingers though, so I rounded 'em up and put 'em in a small box. This bein' the first time I killed anyone. I got a little worried and decided it was time to get movin' with the rest of the plan. I set the finger box aside and leaned in toward her face. She looked at me—eye to fuckin' eye. You know what that whore did?

Nothin' 'cuz I punched her in the face and broke her pretty little jaw! Ha!

She was out cold again. I was pretty much done with her any who, so I grabbed the sheet of plastic I had in the storage and opened it up behind the van and spread it out on the floor. I grabbed the hacksaw and set it in the back of the van while I drug her out by her legs. Once her legs were out of the van, I started with her right leg.

I pressed the saw against her leg and began pushing and pulling it against her skin. Like a hot knife through butter, her skin flayed open. I thought it was gonna be easy the whole time. But I couldn't get that damn saw to bite into her kneecap. That shit was tough. Until I smashed the fuck out of it with a ball-peen hammer anyways.

After that, the lower half of her leg came right off. It was the same way for the other side. Smack, smack, saw, saw. I did the same at her thigh joint but used a crowbar to separate the ball of her femur from the socket.

Oh, after the first lower leg was off, I think she died 'cuz the bitch didn't move. Even when I punched her right in the pussy.

I flipped her around after that and hacked off her arms, first at the elbow, then at the shoulder. As the parts came off, I stacked them in a pile like you would stack logs. Once that was done, I carefully removed her head the same way and set it next to the stack.

This was where I learned a very important lesson. I decided that I wanted to cut her torso in half. Why? Why the fuck not? Fuck that whore... So anyways, I tried to think of the best way to do it and settled on the hack saw.

I made the first cut just below the ribs. What's the worst thing you ever smelled? Well, you ain't never smelled nothin' 'til you cut into a sack of shit! I don't know what this bitch ate, but it smelled like she ate nothin' but hot fuckin' garbage. That shit was ripe.

But I was committed at this point, so I hacked my way through, retching a few times. The strange part was the smell was gross, but I learned the guts didn't bother me. I actually felt accomplished when I got her all taken apart. I felt something, like pride maybe. Whatever. Now here is where shit gets good.

So, I grabbed the paper towels and boxes from the front of the storage. I laid out and separated each body part and gave it a wipe down. I assembled boxes of all sizes. Two of each size actually. I carefully lined each one with plastic. I matched the right size box with the right size limb and sealed a part in each one.

I assembled a perfect head-sized box, re-assembled, and sealed the head inside. Get this... Then I wrapped all the boxes in Christmas paper: Santa paper, Rudolph paper, My Little Pony paper. But the box with the head... I wrapped that in One Direction paper. The perfect paper for the perfect present.

It was almost 3:00 a.m. at that point and I needed to get a move on. I pulled the blood-covered plastic up and bagged it in

Hefty bags. I did the same with the plastic from inside the van and the paper towels too. I bagged the tools. I bagged everything.

I threw all the bags into the van. I grabbed the nipples I had left in the back of the van and tossed them in the finger box. I loaded all the presents into the van. I took special care to load the present with the head in it up front so I could make sure it didn't roll around. It needed to be the perfect present.

I grabbed the last box, marked "Suit," from the front of the storage. I ripped open the top and pulled out its contents. I placed everything in its correct place. Everything had to be right. I was determined to give Suzy the best Christmas ever.

I stripped off all of my clothes right down to my underwear. I scratched my ass as I walked over to the box. I made sure it was empty before I gathered and tossed in all of my bloody clothes. I turned around; a smile filled my face. There, spread in perfect order, was my Santa Suit.

I put each piece on carefully and ensured that I tied every tie and knotted every knot. Everything was going to be great for Suzy. I was sure of it. I tossed the box of old clothes in the van with the hefty bags. The back doors closed with a thud that echoed in the storage. I turned off all of the lights and opened the door.

I backed out and drove straight to Suzy's house, singing Christmas carols the entire way. I was a new man! I sang about packages, boxes, and bags. I sang about everything.

When I pulled into the trailer park I drove the long way around so I could see if the cops were there. To my relief, the lights were still off and a lone candle in the menorah was still burning. I shut off the van's lights and drove to the front of the trailer. I put the van in park and shut off the engine.

This part was going to be tricky. I tiptoed to the front door and, as quietly as I could, propped it open. I slunk down the steps and opened the van doors. I grabbed the boxes full of arms and legs, trunks and torsos, but I saved the best two boxes for last.

I grabbed the box that had the head in it and the finger box. I prominently displayed the head box so it would be the first present Suzy saw. It was the perfect place. I scrawled the perfect note on it:

Suzy,
Open me first!
Merry Christmas,
Santa

What I did next, though, that was just for me. I walked to the still flickering candle, blew it out, and tossed it aside. I removed all the candles. Do you know what I did next? I jammed the fingers in the fucking menorah! It was perfect. Menorah fingers! Seriously— that shit was genius. Fucking menorah fingers!

Can you imagine being the person who finds that? Classic! Anyways, I left that shit up on the counter so Suzy couldn't really see it. No sense traumatizing her on such a joyous day! I also picked up the pussy candle and jammed it in the center holder. I took a minute to look around. Everything looked perfect.

Merry Christmas, kiddo," I said quietly as I walked out the door and closed it behind me.

🕱

Funny feelin' ya get after hackin' up a whore. I remember the next morning—TV programs all over reported this poor kid getting up and un-wrapping her mom's body I took apart. Truth is, that is *kinda* what happened. I imagined it more like this...

The trailer was just startin' to brighten up with the sun rising. Little Suzy opened up her little peepers and immediately filled with Christmas joy! Then poor Suzy remembered that she had to share Christmas with that fuckin' cunt of a mother. The joy quickly left her young heart. But she got up anyway.

Little Suzy searched the house for dear old candle-fuckin' Mommy, but lo and behold! that bitch was nowhere to be found. Suzy stumbled all sleepy-eyed into the living room and bellered something like, "Holy fuck, Santy Clause sure does love me! Look at all these goddamn presents," or whatever kids say these days. HA!

Kids is so sweet and innocent. I imagined that she run over to them presents and hopefully read Santy's note. I'm sure she grabbed the boxes and ripped the Christmas paper off 'em like a tornado ripping through the midwest.

I can just see her bright little eyes when she opened up that perfect little present—the one with Mom's head in it. She musta smiled from ear to ear when she saw that stupid slut was dead. I can almost see her kickin' dear old Mom's head around like a soccer ball. Running from one room to the next kickin' goals.

I assume the cops came when little Suzy got hungry and there wasn't no one to feed her. I shoulda left her a sandwich or something.

Them news people just don't get what a neat thing I did for Suzy. I figured that what I had done was so good, and I wanted to keep doin' it, that I would do it every year for Christmas. Boy, it sure took a while for them news folk to calm down about it. Poor Suzy lost her mommy.

was it. There was no fuckin' way I was gonna let this happen. When good 'ol Donnie Darko hopped back a seat, I grabbed my K- bar and shoved it right in his neck.

Sure, there was some screaming when he sprayed the back seat with his fuckin' blood. Did you know they bleed the same color blood as the rest of us? I learned something new... Ha!

Anyways, I sprung over the seat and wacked that poor little girl's face on the console and she went out like a light. I hope I didn't hurt her too bad.

Then, there were two!

I grabbed the queen-of-the-blowjobs by the hair as she tried to grab for the driver's door. I yanked her back and immediately began delivering a barrage of closed-fist blows to her dick-suckin' lips. I heard some bones cracking as I punched her. I had to get her out before I broke her all up. So, there was always something I wanted to try.

I put that bitch in Sergeant Slaughter's Camel Clutch. I choked the shit out of her WWF style! I couldn't help myself. I started quoting Sergeant Slaughter.

When I'm through, scuzzbucket, they're gonna scrape you off the walls with a squeegee!

I even quoted his lines from the *GI Joe* movie.

This is for Falcon! I punched her in the face.

This is for me! I punched her in the face.

This is for Duke! I punched her in the face.

And this is for the U.S. of A!

I punched that unconscious bitch right in the mother fuckin' tits! Then I started to feel like a goddamn retard, so I threw her on the floor and hopped in the back to finish off the baby-raper. I yanked the K-bar out of his neck and gave him a little stabby-stab to the back of his neck. He was mostly gone before I got back there, but it was a good time anyways. Another sicko pedophile off the street!

I spit on the floor as I looked at my handiwork. That sure when to shit quick. Now I had to un-fuck the mess. Did I mention that I was covered in fuckin' bright-ass red blood? I was soaked. Jesus Christ I was so wet. I used my hand and squeegeed the red liquid off my arms. I wiped the remainder on the second-row seatback.

Ok, the plan was—

First: Get the keys from the whore purse

Second: Drive the fuck-wagon to the storage

Third: Impart some holiday spirit on the slut

Scratch that.

Third: Tie up and gag the poor kid. Can't let her see the surprise early.

Fourth: Impart some holiday spirit on the slut

Fifth: Sedate the kid and deliver the presents

Sixth: Merry Fucking Christmas!

It pretty much went exactly like that. I neglected to mention a few things that wiggled into the plan as well. So I have always wondered what it would be like to curb-stomp someone *American History X* style. The problem was that it looked like that guy got off too easy. This child-whoring-cunt deserved worse. And I had an idea.

After I fed the poor little kiddo a fistful of Benadryl and she was racked the hell out, I drug Mom's still unconscious body out of the van. It just so happened that there was a nice curb near the door to my storage door.

It was nice and dark and I was so pissed it didn't matter. Anyways, I drug her outside. She was bound and gagged, but I needed her awake for what was about to happen. It'd worked so well the first time that, again, I snapped an ammonia inhalant and jammed it up her nose.

Holy fuck, did she wake up fast! Ha!

I could hear her mumbling away through her gag. Whatever. *Enjoy the ability to talk while you can.* I knelt and whispered into her ear. I told her that if she is absolutely silent during what was about to happen, I would let her go.

Obviously, I was full of shit! I ain't letting no baby- pimpin, gutter-slut live. She nodded yes and I untied her gag.

Bite the curb, I told her. She looked at me dumbfounded, like I said it in goddamn French. I leaned in again. "Put your cock-suckin' teeth on the curb—NOW!"

Stupidly, she did. I immediately grabbed her by her hair and placed my knee on the back of her head. I wanted to be close so I could hear this. I moved my hands to either side of her face and pushed my weight slowly onto her head.

Now, I gotta ask, do you know what breaking teeth sound like?

Happy! That's what!

As I pushed down I could actually feel the bone teeth grind down the porous cement curb. Every once in a while, a nice loud crack shot through the air as a tooth broke. She howled like a bitch as blood poured from her mouth and pooled on the curb.

Great, somethin' else to clean up. Today was just full of inconvenience.

Anyway, I had to hurry up 'cuz I had a lot left to do. So I stood up and put a bit more of my wrestling knowledge to work and gave that bitch a Hogan-Leg-Drop. Unfortunately, I missed and slammed my ass cheek right on the back of her head.

Oops—ha!

Her jaw popped right off her face. It sounded like a tree branch snapped. It was awesome! I figured fun time was over and drug her back inside the storage unit.

From there I just did what I did before and hacked her up and put her in presents. With all the crazy shit that happened in the van, I never even got the little girl's name. Oh well.

I delivered the presents dressed as Santa again, just like before. This time, I just left a simple note on the Justin Bieber wrapping paper.

Kiddo,

Merry Christmas!

Santa

Oh—yeah—back to today. I guess the real rookie move was when I lit the van on fire under the bridge. I didn't see that bitch joggin' 'til it was too late. By the time I saw her face lit up by the fire, you stupid motherfuckers were already surrounding me.

By the way, I'm not crazy. I would have complied with anything you told me to do. I don't like cops, but my issue isn't with you. It's really about—You know the real shit thing about this entire deal? I did what I did because I give a shit about them poor kids. I really didn't give a fuck about them Moms. I made them suffer because they deserved to fuckin' suffer. Not them kids.

I don't give a fuck what you or any other motherfucker thinks about me. I gave those kids the perfect presents!

So, ho, ho, fuckin' ho...

Darren leaned back in his chair, rocking it onto two legs. His wrists were bound together by a shiny pair of Peerless handcuffs. He still wore the now badly stained Santa Claus suit. What a mess.

The detective whispered something into his radio and stood.

"Darren, you have a visitor. She says she's your lawyer," the detective said as he moved to the door. "I'll be right outside." The detective walked through the door and nodded at the attorney as she stepped into the room and closed the door. As soon as she turned toward Darren, he could see she was carrying a large, black leather purse. He gasped.

"Mom?" he asked. "How did you—"

"Shh, we don't have much time," she said as she raised a finger to her lips.

"Time for what? I'm in jail," Darren said.

"Oh, you know what I mean, young man," she said with a glimmer in her eye.

Hollie walked to Darren's chair and in seconds had his now stiff rod out. Without missing a beat she climbed onto it and forced its length into her.

"I wanted you to have the perfect present, baby boy," she said as she rode him.

What Darren didn't see was that his mother had grabbed a large-caliber handgun out of her bag. She held it behind his head out of sight as she prepared for the inevitable climax.

Darren's face contorted as he finished inside her.

"I wanted you to have the perfect present. I love you," she said.

A loud *bang* broke the silence of their embrace as the gun fired. Blood splashed on the wall to Darren's right. His body went limp. The door burst open and uniformed police officers flooded the room and took her into custody.

The detective entered right behind them. He surveyed the room. A Santa-suit-clad Darren lay dead on the floor. His cock hung limp outside of the suit bottom and his brains were splashed across the wall.

"What a fucked-up Christmas," he said, shaking his head. Looks like I'll be late tonight. Good thing I got my baby the perfect present.

I WAS A LEGEND

It was early. So—fucking—early. The four members of Raging Wrath stumbled down the jetway and burst into the airport like a hurricane. They all had long, unkempt hair and it was extra ratty from last night's part mixed with their lack of sleep.

Tyler looked at the clock, as he made his way down the hall leading to the people mover. The electronic voice cut off the Bee Gees howling of Staying Alive on the terminal's speakers.

"Welcome to McCarren International Airport. Las Vegas awaits you, please enjoy your stay." A quaint message, he thought. Probably the only quaint thing in this God-damned town. The ear-piercing voice of Barry Gibb returned making his head pound.

"I need some fucking coffee," he said.

"No way brotha," you need a shot!" Micky said.

"Yeah, that too," Tyler stopped abruptly next to the metal trashcan that was conveniently placed in reach of passers-by. He leaned forward, one hand on his stomach and one hand on the cool metallic lip of the lid. With one, very loud retch, he emptied the near neon orange contents of his angry stomach.

"Jesus Christ brotha, that's some rank shit," Mickey said. "You feel better?"

"Yep."

Tyler looked at his sick in horror and wondered what the hell he ate, drank, or took to make it that color. It was defiantly and unnatural vibrant hue. Almost like a construction workers vest.

"Huh... That's— Well that's what you get for listening to the damn Bee Gees," he said smirking.

"So, Mickey, about that shot."

"Aye."

The two flagged down Hurley and Jake and made their way to the closest airport bar. Four stumbles, two trips, and one more vomit session from Tyler and they arrived at McFinnigan's Irish Pub, the self-touted Vegas' #1 Irish Pub. The sign above it said so in obnoxious neon letters.

They approached the bar, pushing past the other patrons sitting near the cut-out meant for one of the few waitresses to pick up drinks. With a waive and a yell Mickey ordered four shots of Jameson with Guinness chasers for the band.

The bartender glanced down at the yelling man. His face lit up in recognition of who the visitors were. Hurridly, he made the ordered drinks and slid them in front of the band.

"For Christ's sake Mickey, I can't start drinking already. I'm puking like the fucking Kool-Aid Man," Tyler said.

"You never stopped drinkin'. Anyway, this is fuckin' Vegas. Sin City, bitch. You can't puss out now!"

He was right. This was Las mother fuckin' Vegas! And he was the singer of the best rock 'n roll band in the world. With that, the shot of Jameson disappeared down his gullet. The shot glass slammed onto the bar.

"To Vegas!" Tyler said raising his pint of Guinness high into the air.

"To Vegas!" the others replied in chorus.

This was already one hell of a tour. Their second. It had been better than any of them had ever expected. Their label, Igneous Records had provided the tour manager with a credit card for "tour expenses." The band had pretty much forced him to buy bottles of booze by the cart load and write them off. Probably not exactly what the label had intended, but hey, rock 'n roll.

They drank several more of the cold brews and once again looked at the manager. A swipe of the card and a quick signature later and they were on their way. Tyler could see the worry on the man's face as he paid for the drinks. He couldn't care less though. This was the rock lifestyle. Excess, sex, drugs, and more sex, and more drugs, and probably even more sex…

Tyler pulled out his iPhone and glanced at it. It was before nine a.m. on a Friday morning. He hated being up so early. Hated seeing other people. Hated having to be "always on" in public. But the beer and liquor helped with that. And the rampant amount of pussy. That helped a lot!

As the group entered the baggage claim area, they were swarmed by fans. This was the worst part. Screams filled the air.

"Oh! There they are! I love you Mickey! I love you Tyler! I love you!" a pack of rabid groupies yelled as they charged the band. *Fuck… Here we go.* Crazed fans shoved Sharpies, photos and CD's at them, all screaming and asking for signatures.

Tyler grabbed whatever items popped directly in front of him, scribbled and returned it back to the fan. He did all of this in complete silence. His head still hurt from the night before and he badly just wanted to leave. But this was part of the gig.

Flash bulbs and smart-phone cameras went off, emitting their now thunderous clicks stealing pieces of the bands privacy with the closing or every shutter. They were surrounded by the mob. Unidentifiable hands jutted out for just a touch of a celebrity.

Some hands were dastardlier than others and found their way to Tyler's crotch. One after the other his cock was groped over and over. The phallus grew with the touches and in no time, was fully erect. He used to fight it, but it was just easier to let it happen. One time, he made the unfortunate mistake of looking down at the hands that stroked him. Only some of them were female and that freaked him out.

He had nothing against queers, but didn't really care for

them touchin' the boom stick. That was for the bitches only! And from that day on, he said he would never look down again. He imagined it was that way for the others too, he couldn't be the only one to look, right?

The band pushed their way toward the doors, eventually making it outside where two black limos awaited them. They made it a rule, after fame had gripped them. Two members per limo. Unlimited groupies. Mickey joined Tyler in his limo while Jake and Hurley got in the other.

They scanned the crowd. The prettiest girls they could reach were pulled into the cars. Some fans begged to be chosen as others were yanked in. Some of the bands security could be seen pushing back the crows and signaling it was time to go.

The lucky few were closed inside the limos with the band. Tyler and Mickey settled into the cool leather seats.

"O.M.G. I can't believe that we are here with you guys! Tyler you are, um… like… amazing. The way you can si—"

"Yeah, yeah. I get it, I'm good. Shut the fuck up and get over here already."

With that Tyler already had his thick black belt undone. A giant silver pentagram belt buckle pulled heavily on the right side of his jeans, splaying them open as he unzipped them. Like an obedient little slut, she was on her knees with his dick pumping in and out of her gagless throat.

Tyler closed his eyes as the woman gobbled hungrily at his tool. *Now this shit, is rock 'n roll!* Ten or so minutes later he glanced over at Mickey who was obviously finished with his girl and was returning his pants, like an airplane tray table, to a full upright and locked position. With one last grunt, he fed the hungry girl her prize. She was a champ too. Gobbled it down without missing a drop.

Buttoning his pants, Tyler rolled down the privacy shade before the girl could get her tits put away and yelled at the driver, "Hey. Pull the fucking car over, would ya?"

"Sure thing sir." His eyes locked on the giant exposed knockers.

Tyler felt the car pull to the side of the road.

"Alright, thanks. Now get the fuck out!" he said motioning the girls to the now open door.

"But this part of town is real bad," she said.

"Well, then I suggest that you hurry before I signal those angry ass niggers over there come and put you to work."

A look of disgust mixed with disbelief spread across her still slobber covered face.

"Jesus, you are an asshole," she said departing the car. She looked in the direction Tyler had nodded and saw four very large black men. "Come on Cheryl, we gotta go."

"Bye honey," Mickey said slapping his girl stiffly on her ass.

"Good bye shugga," she replied.

Tyler watched as the pair scampered off before signaling for the driver to continue to the hotel. As the car pulled away from the curb, the two started up a conversation. It was their first time in Vegas and they wanted to rock and party like they thought rock stars should.

"Can you believe it? Vegas man. Fucking Vegas!" Tyler said.

"Aye man. I canna wait to party. But I need some goddam sleep. I feel like it's been forever since is crashed out."

"It has been two days' man. That's a long ass time. At least we already busted a nut. We can rack out before we party tonight."

"Yeah, I'm gonna drink this fuckin' town dry 'slong as that peckerwood's card keeps-a-workin."

"Same me some, you selfish prick," Tyler laughed.

Before long the limos pulled into the MGM resort. It looked different that he expected. Sure it was green, but it lacked the glitz that only the nighttime lights can provide. It was a good thing they slept during the day. Rock stars were practically vampires that survived on booze, drugs, and pussy instead of blood.

Hotel Managers in suits waited for the vehicles arrival in valet. They were dressed in black suits, complete with ass kissing accoutrements attached. Behind them several baggage attendants stood in a line with carts in hand. Security was close behind them.

The vehicles came to a stop and the band exited. More photographers stood snapping their photos as they stepped out of the vehicles.

The bellmen quickly grabbed luggage from the trunks and loaded their carts.

They made their way into the hotel and went directly to their rooms. The rockers, silent the entire way. The manager stood in the hall as each band member entered their suite. Tyler was the last one to step in. He looked at the dweeby little fuck and yelled to him.

"Tip 'em each a hundo would ya? Thanks."

Before the man had time to reply, the door had closed, with Tyler inside.

Tyler awoke to the sound of his hotel room telephone ringing. He wriggled loosely across the bed and reached for it. He missed, and slid unencumbered to the floor, landing face first where he could only image hundreds of nasty ass feet stood. Where vomit from nights of binge drinking and bachelor parties had splashed. His nose pressed into the carpet... He sniffed. Regret filled him as did the dank foot stink from the carpet. *Why did I...*

The phone rang again. Tyler pushed himself up off the floor and answered the phone with a muffled hello.

"Hey, you fuckin' cunt. Get the fuck up. It's party time. Get your scrawny ass down here," Mickey said.

"Okay, Okay... Just stop yelling."

"Well, hurry up arsehole!"

Tyler hung up the phone, saying nothing else. He stood up, stretching his exhausted rocker body. The mirror across the room reminded him that he slept in all his clothes. Something a man of his age and promiscuity level never does.

He went to the mini-bar and retrieved a Heineken from the refrigerator door, popped its top, and took a big slug of it. Heineken was one of his least favorite beers. Mostly because it smelled and tasted like a skunk's ass smells.

He wasn't going to let that kind of petty bullshit get in the way of getting his party started. He grabbed a second one and made his way to the shower. With a twist of the dial he turned the water on as hot as he could stand it. While he waited, he stripped off his clothes and while still outside, began peeing into the shower.

The room filled with the stink of his now steaming hot piss as it mixed with the hot water. The relief was incredible. The stream came to an end after a couple last squirts. He sniffed.

"Smells like excellence!"

He often joked that his piss smelled like excellence with his band-mates, a joke not requiring company to make on this night. *What the fuck is wrong with me?* He snickered, stepping into the water.

"You're not supposta let this kinda shit happen you worthless little fuck!" Mickey yelled at the manager. Wha' the fuck do you mean the band owes $300,000 in "tour expenses?" I thought that's wha' they gave you the goddam card for," Mickey said.

"Mickey, the label is fucking pissed that you guys bought booze, coke, and all kinds of other bullshit with it. It was supposed to be for legit expenses," the manager said.

"That's nah our problem you little weasel. You are in control of tha' card. Na' us. That makes it your problem."

"Unfortunately not. It is the band problem. One that the label wants to get fixed now."

"How in da' fuck are we supposed to just shit out $300k? My arse look like an ATM to you?

"Obviously not. But That's something you and the others are going to have to figure out. I'm glad to help any way I can but the bosses know that you made me use this card against my wishes. They know that I didn't want to spend $300,000 dollars."

"You are one worthless piece of—"

A knock sounded at the door.

"Na' a word of this to anyone else. I'll tell 'em myself. Now get the fuck out of my room. I don't wanna see ya until show time tomorrow. I'm not even sure I wanna see ya then!"

"Alright Mickey. Let me know if there is anything I can do to help okay?"

"Piss off."

With that, the manager stood up and walked to the door, opening it. Jake and Hurley stood on the other side.

"What up worm?" Jake, the bands base player asked.

The manager scowled and pushed through the pair, departing without a word.

"What's up the Penguin's ass?" Jake asked.

"Little fucker says we owe the label $300k for expenses and they want it real soon or they are gonna pull us off tour and void our contract."

"What the fuck? They can't do that. He thinks that just because he looks like Danny DeVito in Batman that he can be a tough guy and rip us off? No fuckin' way."

"No matter what, I know that Tyler is gonna be pissed. Who wants to tell him?" Mickey asked.

"No way bro!" Hurley said.

"He's your best buddy dude," Jake said.

"Shite. I knew your pricks were gonna fuck me over. Fine, I'll do it. You two retards better go enjoy Vegas while you can. Don't think we'll be joinin' ya."

"Sorry dude. Good luck! Let us know what you guys decide," Jake said.

"Aye. Now get lost. Quick."

As quick as they appeared, they were gone. It wasn't long before Tyler arrived. He was clad in black leather pants, black boots, and a half buttoned black button up.

"Brotha, you goin' to a funeral? It's Vegas not Death Valley."

"Bite me shithead. Where are the guys? Let's get this party started. Where's the weasel? We need a little cha-ching."

"He won't be joinin' us tonight. Somethin's come up. Let's go get some Jack and we'll talk about it."

"Oh hell. This can't be good."

"Nah so much. Shit'll work itself out though."

The pair of rockers snuck down to the giftshop and bought a couple bottles of Jack Daniels before returning to the elevators.

"Hey Mickey, let's go outside. Sit on the top floor of the garage. No offence but your room smells like dirty feet."

"I've got your dirty feet right here," he said as he kicked Tyler in the ass.

The two made their way to the garage eventually finding the elevators and hearing to the top floor. Once outside, they found a ledge that had the best view of "The Strip" and hopped up on it, dangling their feet over the edge.

Mickey spent the next little bit explaining what he was told by their manager. He told him how the weasel was trying to dodge all responsibility even though he was the one using the card and signing for it. He told him everything.

"This is really fucked man," Tyler said as he took another mouthful of Jack.

"Aye, but what are we gonna do?"

"I don't know yet," Tyler said. "I Have no fucking clue. I need to go for a walk. I can't think," he said taking another drink.

"You want me to come with ya'?"

"Nope."

That was it, one word and Tyler stood up and walked away.

Not wanting to be with people, Tyler walked away from Las Vegas Boulevard and made his way to where the locals live. What he didn't realize is just how shady the area behind the strip is. Before long he was in an area that looked vaguely familiar to him.

Oh, yeah, this is where we dumped the whores. He chucked thinking about how he just kicked them out of the car. How he told them to get out before the niggers pimped 'em out. He looked around drinking more of the bitter liquor.

The bottle was half gone already and his head was starting to spin. Must have been the heat. He wasn't used to it and it was totally fucking with his tolerance. He felt like a kid again. It had been a long time since just a half of a bottle got him woozy.

And what was up with all the lights? Someone needs to turn Vegas off once in a while. Damn power bills must be crazy. He took his thoughts and headed down an alley in search of a darker, less blinding spot.

Several minutes later he found himself standing in front of Rita's Tarot. There was a sign in the window that said, guaranteed to solve your problems. First reading free.

That's all it took to win over the intoxicated men. He had a problem, and this apparently, was a place with a solution. And it was free.

He took another large gulp from his bottle and staggered in. A small chime dinged when he passed through the door. The room inside was nearly as dark as the alley. Only a few small candles lit its sprawling interior.

"Welcome to Rita's," a female voice said. "Please, come in. I am Rita, how may I help you?"

"Hi Rudy," he said, knowingly messing up her name, but not caring.

"Rita."

"Fine. Rita. I got a problem, and it's a big one."

"Well, we have solutions. All you have to do is sit, and we can get started."

Tyler carefully made his way to the chair, not wanting to fall over. He slid it out, moved in front of it and plopped down. A sharp pain ripped through his right ass cheek making him jump to his feet.

"Ouch, what the hell is that?" he asked.

"Oh my. Turn around dear. Let Rita have a look."

He felt around for the cause of the pain but couldn't find it. He decided that he better let Rita have a look. He turned around and Rita moved closer with a candle. She placed her hand on his right butt cheek and rubbed it.

"Hey, lady. I came here to solve a problem, not get a felt up by some two-bit fortune teller."

Rita pulled at the leather seat of his pants and came away with something causing him to yell out in pain.

"My apologies. I was not trying to feel up your butt. I was trying to find this. There was a loose staple in the chair. It seemed to have popped through your pants and stuck into your flesh."

Rita held the staple up, showing it to Tyler and apologizing again.

"Please have a seat. Let us get to your real problem. Let me get you a more comfortable chair.

Rita stood and retrieved a black, mesh bottomed chair from the next room. She quickly swapped it out with the rickety wooden one Tyler had first sat in.

"Please, please." Rita motioned toward the chair.

Tyler sat cautiously in the new chair, his ass still throbbed from the pain. Rita returned to her seat and retrieved a glass ball from under the round table. She set it on a small pedestal in the center of the circle.

"Shall we begin?"

"Shall we begin?" Tyler mocked. "No I want to sit around all fucking night. Cut the hocus pocus bullshit and let's put your guarantee to the test."

In Tyler's head, he had already decided that there was nothing this Rita bitch could do for him and it was she was just a fraud. The funny thing was, in a moment of drunken clarity, he thought, a guarantee is a guarantee. If she doesn't do what is advertised, that is false advertising and grounds for a lawsuit. He hoped a $300,000 lawsuit!

"Very well. But please, be courteous to Rita, for I am but a humble servant, here to help."

"I'm sorry Rita."

"Tell me what problem you have that needs fixing. But be careful in your requests, as everything comes with a price."

"Ooh, everything comes with a price. Blah, blah, blah. Okay Rita. My problem is I'm too goddam drunk to believe a fucking thing you say. Not to mention, I can barely think let alone solve a doozy of a problem."

"Very well. As the sign says, the first is free. Place your hands on the ball."

He did as she said and Rita quickly covered his hands with hers. He locked eyes with her as she began to mumble in a language that he couldn't understand.

"Shoklavesh. Salazkaar. Incultaan."

She repeated the phrase over and over, growing louder each time. The room glowed with light emitting from the ball under their hands. The light grew brighter as she grew louder until— Silence.

"Look that was a neat parlor trick and all, but I don't have time for you or your fancy lightbulb. Okay?"

Tyler stood, jerking his hands back from Rita, and turned toward the door, determined to leave.

"Are you still too drunk to understand Rita?" she asked.

Tyler took a step toward the door. Not a staggered step. An actual, steady, planned step. Holy shit. He was sober.

"How did you do that? What is there something with the light that burns off alcohol?"

"You asked for the problem to be fixed. Rita fixed it. Do you have more problems?"

"Holy shit! Yeah I have fucking problems."

"Rita will fix them for you. Just remember, everything has a price."

"Baby, if you can fix my problems, then money won't be a problem."

"Please sit, let us begin again. What would you like help fixing?"

"Okay. Look, I gotta see if this is real. You understand, don't you? Before I can give you any money, I have to see if you can fix something a bit more real than my drunkenness."

Rita nodded. "I will fix any problem. Just remember, everything has a price."

"Yeah ok, whatever. Let's see how good you are. Rita, I have a problem. I walked down here but I'm too lazy to walk back to my hotel."

"What is the problem?" Rita asked.

"The problem is I don't have a 2013 Audi Nanuk Quattro to drive back to my hotel. That, is my problem."

"Very well. Place your hands on the ball." Again, the room began to glow with light from the ball as Rita chanted. "Shoklavesh. Salazkaar. Incultaan."

Several seconds later, the chanting and glowing ceased. Tyler looked at Rita.

"Well, where is my car?"

"Your problem is solved," she said, nodding at the window.

Tyler sprang to his feet. "Holy shit. There, outside the building sat the car of his dreams.

"You know that is a $5,000,000 concept car, right?"

"I do. Did I solve your problem?"

"Yeah you did! Oh, my God!"

"No! You will not speak of any God in here! Rita is the fixer. The only one you need. The one that solves your problem. Not some God!"

"Whoa, okay. I'm sorry. There is no God, only Rita," he said, mocking Ghostbusters.

"Do you believe me now? Do you have another problem in need of fixing?"

Tyler couldn't believe what was happening. How could this little lady, which, by the way, he had yet to get a good look at, do these amazing things? A $5,000,000 car. Just given to him. This was unbelievable.

May as well fix the real problem of the $300,000 debt to the stupid label.

"Yeah, I have a problem that needs fixing Rita."

"Sit, please tell me about your problem."

Tyler told Rita of the money problems. The debt his band owed the record label. The shitty manager trying to screw them out of the money. He vented for twenty minutes to Rita.

He struggled to try and get a better look at her while he talked. No such luck though. It was damn dark in the room and each time the ball lit with light, it blinded him so he couldn't see her.

"What is the problem you need fixed? Be specific if you want Rita to help. But remember, everything has a price."

Man, this woman really went on about things having a price. Yeah, I heard you the first time you old bag... Jesus Christ.

"You will not bring up a God in here. You will not speak of it, or think of it again. Rita will not tolerate insolence. Rita will not tell you again. Do you understand?"

"Yes ma'am." *How did she know?*

"Do you have anything that requires fixing? But remember everything has a price."

"Yeah. I do. I tell you what. You keep the car and just give me the $5,000,000 cash. That should take care of my bands problem."

"Very well. Your hands please."

He presented her with his hands and she placed them on the ball. Longer this time the light pulsed and she chanted.

"Shoklavesh. Salazkaar. Incultaan."

I wonder what that means. Who cares? It means I'm gonna be rich! That's what it means!" Like before, the chanting eventually stopped. Tyler filled with excitement as he looked around the room. There was no money. He looked out the window. The car was gone too.

"What's your game Rita? Where is the $5,000,000? Where is the car? Are you just fucking with me?"

"Rita is the fixer. You have your money and like you told me to do, I took the car back."

"Where is the money? I don't see it."

Rita handed Tyler the newspaper. A photo on the cover shows him at the MGM standing in front of a slot machine holding a check for $5,000,000. The headline reads, "Famous Frontman of Raging Wrath Hits It Big at the MGM!"

"I'm supposed to believe this?"

"Rita does not lie. Check your back account. The money is there."

"The banks are closed. How am I supposed to—my phone!"

Tyler plunged his hand into his pants pocket and retrieved his cell. As fast as possible, he opened his banking app. What he saw nearly killed him. Available Balance: $5,032,374.19. *Holy shit... It's real.*

Tyler tried to slide his phone back into his pocket. Jittering with nervous energy, he slipped from the chair and landed on his butt.

Right where the staple had pricked him. An unbelievable amount of pain shot through his body causing him to scream.

"Fuck! I think this staple might have got me better than I thought."

He reached behind and touched his ass cheek. Crippling pain jolted through his body. He dropped to one knee and looked at his hand. It was dripping with blood.

"Holy crap! Rita, I have to go get this looked at."

With that he pulled his phone out of his pocket and hit the power button.

"What's the address here?"

Rita pointed to the window where the address was displayed. He nodded and raised his phone up, hitting the power button again. Nothing.

"Shit it's dead. Rita, Can I use your phone?"

"Rita is a fixer," she said pointing at the phone on the wall. It was the old kind with the long spiral cord. "Just remember, everything has a price."

Tyler ran to the phone and lifted the receiver, putting it to his ear. He dialed 911 on the base and listened. The phone rang once before it was answered by the dispatcher.

"911, what's your emergency?"

"I'm bleeding. I'm bleeding a lot. I need an ambulance," Tyler said.

"Okay sir, please calm down. What's your address?"

"I'm at 666 Paradise Road. I'm at Rita's Tarot Shop. Please hurry."

"Very funny sir. This is the one-hundredth call from that place this week. That isn't a real address and that isn't a real place. Please stop calling the police. Reporting a false crime is a felony sir." The phone clicked as the dispatcher hung up.

"Rita, what's going on? Why did the police say this is a fake place and a fake address?"

"Rita is a fixer. Do you have a problem that needs fixing?"

"Yeah... Jesus Christ, Rita. My ass is pouring blood and I want that to stop. Oh, and while we are at it, I want to be famous. A legend. Can you make that happen? For God's sake, you are one crazy ass bitch!"

Rita stood and howled in rage. "I warned you," she said. Rita stepped from her side of the table. As she stepped closer to Tyler, her image faded. There in front of Tyler stood a portly man. Tyler looked him up and down. The man wore royal looking attire from the olden days. He carried a staff now and had cloven feet, like that of a very large deer.

"What the fuck are you?" Tyler asked.

His face shown the terror that wretch inside him. His body shook and reeled with nausea. The beast stepped closer.

"Your hands," it said.

Tyler did not give up his hands. "No." I don't want you to touch me. He scrambled backwards toward the door. He turned and gave the nob a twist.

"It's too late Tyler. Come to Nybbas and let me show you what is happening."

"What the fuck is Nybbas?" Tyler said through his terror.

"I am Nybbas. I am the demon that you turned to in your time of need, Tyler. I am he who helped give you the solutions to your problems. I am he who will, unfortunately be your end."

"My end? Yes. You see, you have asked for more that your soul has to give Tyler. Look under your seat."

Tyler knelt and looked. A pentagram on a large seal of the underworld was clearly visible now. The thing was soaked in blood. His blood.

"You see Tyler, you asked me for a great many things. Wondrous things. And I warned you that everything has a price. Did I not?"

"Yeah you did but…"

"No Tyler. There is no but. These things are very clear. I told you of the fee each time you asked for something else. Don't fret though. You have accomplished a great many things in your time on earth. Why just tonight, you won $5,000,000 dollars. Someone is going to get your money. Who did you leave your earthly belongings to?"

"No one. I didn't have anyone to leave them to. I didn't think I needed a will."

"Oh a poor choice. What a terrible mistake. I am not a vile being though. Please, have a seat. Let me show you some things."

Tyler sat in his chair as Nybbas returned to his seat.

"I'm afraid I will need your hands again though. That's how this silly ball works."

Reluctantly, Tyler placed his hands on the ball at the center of the table. This time the ball disappeared and Tyler found himself standing with Nybbas at the MGM.

"You see Tyler, when you asked for your blood to stop leaking from your and to be a legend, that simply cost more than you had to offer."

"Cost what?"

"Of course, I am sorry. Your soul Tyler. Each drop of blood contains a piece of your soul. The more you asked for, the more of your soul it cost and the more I took. The car, the money… each took some, but little in comparison to changing your status in life. You see, to change you into a legend, I must take bits of the will of others and give them to you. That isn't a problem if I have others willing to give it to me. It's just a bit of an inconvenience. "

"What fucking good is giving it to me if I can't enjoy it?"

"Your enjoyment is not my concern. I am here to fix things and collect souls. Like I said though, I am not a diabolical creature. I could have just taken your soul after it was cashed out and forgot about your problems. That is not my style. Come, let me show you."

Nybbas escorted Tyler down to the casino where the band was hanging out with the weasel. They were all laughing and drinking. They appeared to be the happiest they had ever been. Mickey started to talk so Tyler and Nybbas hushed.

"Can you believe this? Tyler won $5 mil tonight, then the bloody damn record label calls, forgives our debt and all because Tyler is an overnight, millionaire rock star? There are fans surroundin' the damn casino right now tryna' get a look at him. Every goddam tabloid has called me tonight askin' for a quote."

"You see Tyler, I am not all bad. Sure, it may have cost you your soul but look at the happiness you have brought to your bandmates. You're a legend in their eyes. I tell you what I'm gonna do for you

Tyler. I'm gonna let you pick someone to give all your money to. I'll make up a will and put it in the safe at your house. Who ya gonna pick? Got a lovely lady at home? A daughter maybe? Or maybe one of the boys in the band? It'd be a shame to watch all that money go nowhere and die in limbo. What'll it be?

"I don't have anyone at home. Just an empty apartment. No family, parents are long dead. I guess Mickey should have it."

"Ah, a wise choice. A very wise choice. Consider it done. Can I tell you a little secret?"

"I guess so."

"You would have been a huge rock star. Bigger than any there's ever been. But you had to go piss it away. Had to get greedy. You had to be an asshole. Those two ladies that gave you a bit of pleasure this afternoon. The came runnin' in to see 'ol Rita. Seems they got kicked out of a limo in a nasty part of town.

"They said some rock star, I'm assuming that's you, kicked them out and told them get goin' for them niggers put 'em to work. They ran into my shop screaming how four big black fellas were chasing them. 'Ol Rita got right on the case. Said they had a problem with you that needed—fixin'.

"Anyways, I let them use my phone. They called 911. Funny thing is 911 couldn't find my address. But I put a little of their will in you. The will to come find me. Looks like it all worked out.

Tyler, it's been a grand time, but I have to get back to my little shop. I have to be a lawyer tomorrow. Some rock star named Mickey discovered that a legend left him a fortune. He's gonna come see me to collect."

"Good thing I won't be alone," Tyler said shaking his head. "At least, I was a legend."

ABOUT THE AUTHOR

 Mathew Kaufman is an American author primarily known for writing in the horror, fantasy, and young adult genres. Mat is a longtime writer for the Never Fear horror series alongside New York Times bestselling authors F. Paul Wilson and Heather Graham and many more.

Mat has also been featured in the first ever Romantic Times Anthology, Romantic Times: Vegas and the follow up RT Haunted West. Mathew lives in Las Vegas, NV and when he isn't writing also works as a Paramedic.

MathewKaufman.com